# ENCHANTRESS OF CRUMBLEDOWN

# ENCHANTRESS OF CRUMBLEDOWN

## DONALD R. MARSHALL

CINNAMON
TREE™

Published by
Deseret Book Company
Salt Lake City

Library of Congress Catalog Card Number 90-81830

ISBN 0-87579-352-5

Printed in the United States of America

10   9   8   7   6   5   4   3   2   1

*For*
*Robin, Jordan, and Reagan*
*—and to all the Cassies of the world*

# 1

They looked at first like three drowned birds washed up on the bank of a river. But it really wasn't a riverbank, and they weren't three little birds at all; they were three drenched and shivering children, waiting by the edge of a wet gray highway.

For a moment they stood watching the road and hugging themselves while the rain poured down their faces and made their hair stick even closer to their wet cheeks. Then suddenly a large gray truck appeared out of nowhere, its canvas covering flapping in the wind as it roared by. With a squeal the children scurried down off the side of the road, slipping and sliding into a small muddy gully. There, they huddled together, their teeth chattering and their bodies shaking in the cold.

"*Please*, let's go back," begged Brittany, the smallest of the two girls.

"No," whimpered the boy. "Please—let's not go back." He was little, not much more than six.

"But it's *so* cold," the girl Brittany went on pleading as she rocked her shivering body back and forth. She was about eleven, but considerably smaller than the thirteen-year-old Ashley beside her, who still didn't speak but steadily kept her eyes on the road running along the top of the embankment beyond.

The boy—"Tiger" they called him although his real name was Theodore—looked up at them again. Rainwater dripped off his nose and chin, and his mouth quivered. "I'm not going back," he said, ducking his head and shaking it back and forth over and over. "I'm not ever going back, no matter what."

Brittany looked at Ashley, impatient for her to make the decision, yet knowing in her heart that if Ashley did say they had better go back, it wouldn't really be the answer she longed for. All she wanted was to be somewhere that was warm.

She thought about the Oglethorpes' house where they had been staying for the last eight or nine months, and she felt a little shiver different from the ones caused by the rain dripping down her neck. She remembered the dank smell of the family room downstairs—a musty smell that came partly from the fact that the Oglethorpes kept a gigantic German shepherd dog that slept on the worn couch or on the rug under the green ping-pong table; she remembered too the kitchen where one of the fluorescent bulbs always seemed to flicker and the refrigerator was off limits unless Mrs. Oglethorpe was in there to supervise; and she remembered the Oglethorpes themselves. Not bad as far as foster parents go—although it always seemed strange to Brittany that she and Ashley and Tiger had to eat their meals on the stools at the counter while the Oglethorpes and their four children — as tall and pale and skinny as the parents themselves — got to sit at the big table that not only had a white tablecloth, but also all the serving bowls of food so they could help themselves without even having to ask.

She looked at Ashley and Tiger. Luckily, they had each other. And even though Tiger was getting to be more and more of a problem, getting into their things all the time now and wanting to play whatever they were playing, even if it was Barbies or something like that, she wished that he was *her* brother and not Ashley's. Or she wished that she and Ashley were real sisters and not just foster sisters as they had been since last September. Or, most of all, she wished that her own brother Rob could be with her — even though he was fifteen now and didn't have much use for a fourth-grade sister. She hadn't seen him since they had been split up by the Child Protection Center last fall, except for about five minutes one day in January when he had ridden by the school playground on his bike and brought her a late Christmas present — some bookends that he'd made in his high school wood-working class.

"What are we going to do?" Tiger was asking.

Brittany stared at Ashley. *If only Rob were here, he would know what to do,* Brittany thought. It made her feel even colder and sadder to think that, not only was her big brother not here, but she didn't even know where he was. All he had told her last January was that he didn't really like the family he was living with and that the social workers were probably going to transfer him. She didn't understand why they couldn't have been placed together in the same foster home. After all, "We try not to split up brothers and sisters," Mrs. Pollock, the supervisor, had told them three years ago. But last summer, after they had the bad experience with the Millers, she had been sent to live with the Oglethorpes and Rob had been placed somewhere else—possibly, Brittany thought, because he had been getting into a lot of trouble stealing things, and the social workers had thought he would be a bad influence on her.

"Okay, come on, let's go," Ashley announced, suddenly standing up straight in the rain. "But we'd better stay down off the road because, if anyone sees us, we're goners."

"Where are we going?" Tiger asked, trailing behind.

"Somewhere. Just don't let anybody see us. And if they do—I mean, if a truck stops or something—just let me do the talking. We have to look like we know where we're going."

"But where *are* we going?" Brittany wanted to know.

Ashley swallowed. "Just follow me." She hoped they wouldn't notice any sound of fear or hesitation in her voice. *Somebody* had to be the leader. And she *had* been out this way before—sort of. At least she had driven by several times—well, a time or two—with the Oglethorpes. Wasn't this the way to Littlefield or Fairmont? Or was Fairmont way out on the *other* side of town?

It had been her idea to get off the school bus where they did. The only problem was, Mr. Ridley, the bus driver, had noticed they were getting off too early, and she had had to call back something quick and made up. (What had she said? Something like "We're invited to a party" — and then she had had to jerk Tiger out of the door before he had time to ask, "We *are?* What party?") It wasn't that they hadn't talked about running away; it was just that they had never planned to do it today — least of all, in the rain. But it had suddenly seemed to Ashley like a perfect time — well, almost perfect. At least none of the Oglethorpe children had been there to tell on them, since Dewey, who happened to be the only one who still rode the elementary school bus, had luckily stayed home with what he claimed was a bad cold. She only wished that Mr. Ridley hadn't noticed, because now, when the Oglethorpes finally realized that the three of them had never come home on the bus, the bus driver would tell them where they had gotten out.

"The important thing," Ashley found herself saying aloud, "is to get as far away as we can from where we got off the bus."

They had already walked what seemed like three miles, although she was afraid it wasn't really that far. In fact, when she looked back over her shoulder, she thought she could still see the sign, a speck of white way down the road, that would say "ENTERING CHESTERTON" on one side and "LEAVING CHESTERTON" on the other.

A car was coming down the road from the direction of town. Ashley pulled the collar of her windbreaker up around her chin and turned her back to the car. "C'mon," she said, giving the other two children a little nudge to keep moving forward.

An icy feeling slithered down her back. The car was stopping. "Keep walking," she ordered in a coarse whisper. Out of the corner of her eye, she was aware that someone in the car seemed to be rolling down the window and partly leaning out.

"Where are you going?" a woman's voice called.

"Don't look back!" Ashley ordered, putting her arms around the other two and shepherding them forward.

"Hellooooo!" the woman called again. "Can I give you a ride? You're going to be all wet."

*Going* to be all wet! They had been drenched five minutes after they had left the bus. "Just keep walking," Ashley whispered firmly.

Two long honks came from the car, and the woman called out again: "I can give you a ride if you want."

Ashley stopped all of a sudden and turned around. "No, thanks, we're just—"

"What?" the woman called out. "Can I take you somewhere?"

Ashley hesitated, then suddenly nudged the others

toward the car. Brittany stared at her in unbelief as she heard Ashley's voice call out hoarsely, "Where are you going?"

The woman's voice was difficult to hear above the rain, but she seemed to be shouting something like: "I'm going to Paley's Crossing—eleven miles down the road. Where do you live?"

Both Brittany and Tiger stared at Ashley, who seemed to take a deep breath then call back, "We're just going down the road. We're—we're visiting some friends . . . "

"Well, come and get in and I'll take you."

For a moment they all hesitated, then the two smaller children felt Ashley's hands pushing them from behind in the direction of the car. "Just let *me* talk," she whispered.

The lady was leaning over the seat, holding the door to the back open for them when they reached the shiny-wet car. Just as Ashley touched the door handle, lightning flashed somewhere and she pulled her hand back quickly, wondering if it was a bad omen of some sort. Never accept a ride with strangers, grown-ups had warned her. (*Especially if you're trying to run away!* she told herself—only no one had ever mentioned *that* part.)

"Hurry, get in. You're all soaked."

Ashley reluctantly helped Tiger in, then she and Brittany followed, all of them perching on the edge of the back seat like three frightened sparrows. The middle-aged lady at the wheel looked back at them. "Now where is it you need to get to?"

"Uh—where did you say you were going?" Ashley finally managed to squeak out.

"Me? I'm going all the way to Paley's Crossing. Just came into town to shop," the lady said, motioning to the sacks and boxes of groceries beside her in the front seat. "I'm Mrs. Finlayson. We have a farm just north of Paley's Crossing."

"Well, we're sort of going that way too," Ashley said. Then, adding quickly: "To a birthday party."

"Oh?" the lady asked, sounding puzzled. "And you were going to walk all the way? In the rain? Whose house?"

Brittany stared at Ashley, terrified, wondering what on earth she was going to say. When Ashley didn't answer but just looked pale and sick, Brittany closed her eyes tight, repeating to herself over and over, *I'm glad it's her, not me. I'm glad it's her, not me.* She only wished, though, that she didn't feel as if she had to go to the bathroom so desperately.

"I forget the name," Ashley was saying. "I mean the last name—but I'm pretty sure I'll know the house when I see it. It's not far from the road."

The next ten minutes were probably the longest ten minutes that any of the three of them had experienced. Even Tiger sat nervously on the edge of the seat watching out of the window on both sides for a farmhouse that might look like there could be a party going on inside where they would be welcome. Ashley was glad that when she told the lady they were the Frankweiler children—a name that happened to pop into her mind because of a book she had read—the lady didn't ask any more questions but simply said there were a lot of families in Chesterton that she didn't know. And Brittany tried to count the telephone poles in order not to think about how hard her heart was pounding.

"That's it!" Ashley shouted suddenly as they approached a white farmhouse.

"Why, that's the Buellers. I didn't know that they had any children that would be—"

"Wait!" Ashley gulped. "Keep going. It must a house *like* that." Through the windshield wipers, she could see two or three other farmhouses up ahead. She felt sick. What if none of them looked at all like the one they had just passed? What if Mrs. Finlayson knew all of the families and none of them had any children? She read a name on a mailbox they passed: Fairbourn. Dare she try it?

Suddenly she saw a little dirt road up ahead that led off to the left. Not far down the road was a tiny frame house with green shutters.

"Who lives there?" she asked quickly.

"Now that one I don't know—" Mrs. Finlayson started to say.

"That's it!" Ashley cried out. "Just let us off at the corner."

"But are you sure it's the right one? I don't want to just drop you off out in the middle of—"

"Positive!" Ashley said. "Aren't you?" she asked, turning to Brittany and giving her a quick pinch on the leg.

"Ouch—yes," Brittany said, squirming.

"It is?" Tiger asked, almost convinced that the two girls had been there before.

The car came to a stop at the corner. The rain seemed to have let up suddenly, and the girls almost fell over each other as they clambered out of the stuffy car and into the fresh cool air outside. The fields looked intensely green, and the house, though they had never seen it before in their lives, was a welcome sight. They all thanked Mrs. Finlayson and waved vigorously as she drove hesitatingly away. Without a word they marched down the dirt road toward the farmhouse, glancing back over their shoulders to make sure that Mrs. Finlayson's car was long out of sight. Then, almost instantaneously, they broke into a run, passing the house as they fled down the road, dodging mud puddles as they went. Ashley ran ahead, Brittany following close behind and so relieved to be out of the car that she didn't even stop to wonder where they were going next.

Huffing and puffing, Tiger scampered along behind. "Hey, wait, you guys!" he called out. "What about the *party?*"

Down the road they ran, the air moist and cool against their hot cheeks. Except for an occasional cow in the fields or a bird fluttering up from a fence post, no one was in sight. Only the fresh green stretched out for miles on each side of them.

It was Ashley who stopped first, panting. "Let's rest," she managed to gasp.

Brittany caught up with her but could only nod in agreement until she got her breath. Head down, Tiger torpedoed toward them, almost knocking both of them down as he crashed into them. "I'm dying!" he breathed, dramatically.

For a moment they all three stood there in the middle of the road, struggling for breath as they looked at one another's straggly-damp hair and mud-spattered legs.

"*Now* what do we do?" Brittany finally asked. "I'm so *wet.*"

"Well," Ashley said, her eyes darting quickly around her in search for a clue, "we . . . need to go a little further . . . to make sure nobody'll find us."

She turned and looked down the road ahead. Not far away a row of tall skinny trees stretched across the field to the left, making her think there might be another road there.

"Follow me," she announced.

"But what are we going to do?" Brittany asked. "Are we going to have to sleep in the fields tonight?"

"No!" Tiger begged. "Not in the fields! There might be yucky things—like snakes and stuff."

Ashley glared at her brother. "Just go back then, if you want. I never said running away would be easy."

She continued walking, keeping her eyes on the string of trees ahead, relieved that both Tiger and Brittany were following close behind, despite an occasional whimper. *Neither of them would dare go back,* she told herself. Certainly not without *her*—and, more than likely, not even *with* her. She could picture them both breaking into tears if she were to suddenly stop and announce that they were all going back to the Oglethorpes.

Not that it would be that bad—for her, at least. She had adopted a method of gritting her teeth and accepting whatever happened. Life wasn't meant to be one circus after another, anyway—although, if she had her way, she would certainly consider making it more of a carnival than it had turned out to be. But life at the Oglethorpes' was at least no worse than it had been at home—and probably better.

She cringed to think of the nights, long before the Oglethorpes, when her real mother would come home after midnight to the big brick apartment house in Rupert

City and wake her up by throwing things and screaming. Once she had ripped down the shower curtain and smashed the bathroom mirror with a bottle. Another time, she had brought a man home with her, and ended up by throwing a pair of scissors at him that even stuck up in the back of his leg, and then she had sat down in the middle of the floor and cried the rest of the night.

For almost as long as Ashley could remember, it had been her job to take care of Tiger. Sometimes a lady with a screaming baby of her own had come and watched after them, but many days Ashley had had to stay home from school, searching for leftovers in the fridge for the two of them to eat and trying to find something to use for Tiger's diaper when the dresser drawers became empty and the damp, reeking pile in the bathtub grew higher and higher.

No, life at the Ogelthorpes' was certainly better than *that* had been. But it really wasn't *home* for her or Tiger. They had both felt like outsiders—permitted to peek in but not touch. "Don't let me ever catch you getting into the cupboards unless I've told you to get something," Mrs. Oglethorpe had warned. And: "We don't allow things from downstairs to be brought upstairs." Or: "You have no business going into the children's rooms. Those are off limits." Like the front room. Or the parents' bedroom. Or the tool shed. "I don't care what Dewey did," she could still hear Mrs. Oglethorpe saying. "What I let Dewey do is no business of yours."

Ashley gave her head an abrupt little shake as if to make the unpleasant thoughts of the Oglethorpes disappear, realizing that they had already reached the spot where the tall trees lined a narrow dirt road leading off to the left and eventually into what looked like a deep green woods.

"Are we going down there?" Tiger asked, hesitating.

"Yes," Ashley announced, trying to make her body very tall as she turned into the tiny lane.

"And sleep in those trees way down there? On the wet ground?" He scrunched his shoulders uncomfortably, picturing himself curling up into a shivering little ball on the muddy forest floor. Brittany, too, envisioned the three of them huddled together under a covering of decayed leaves just like in a sad picture she had seen once called *Babes in the Woods*.

"Maybe we can find a barn or something," Ashley said. But there seemed to be no barns or farmhouses or signs of human life of any kind, and the narrow lane they had been walking down was becoming so overtaken with weeds that it seemed scarcely more than two little cow trails. "I don't like it down here," Tiger whispered. Thick clusters of trees loomed on both sides of the road, with dark green vines covering the trunks and hanging down from the branches overhead.

"Maybe we should go back," Ashley said softly. But then she noticed a spot further on where the last rays of the sun slanted through the trees enough to catch a spot of rich yellow-green in the tall grass beyond.

They all moved on, almost as if something invisible were pulling them through the dusky glen. And when the trees and vines finally thinned enough to expose the grassy clearing beyond, they all stopped.

The setting sun cast everything in a mellow amber glow. And in the midst of the tall wild grass, almost lost in a tangle of weeds and deep-green vines, was a little stone house. It looked sadly neglected and tumbledown: some of the windows were boarded up, some were partly broken out, and the weathered door hung crookedly from a single hinge. Still, it was the closest thing to a picture-book cottage that any of them had ever seen — and all so lost in such a heavy overgrowth of vines that even the cottage itself seemed to grow up out of the grass.

For a second they stood there breathless. In their hearts, they all knew it; they didn't even need Ashley to say it. But she said it anyway: "This . . . ," she whispered half aloud. "This is were we're going to live!"

Even as they stood entranced in front of the vine-encrusted cottage, the rosy light faded and a dusky shadow seemed to creep over the house.

Tiger shuddered. "What if it belongs to somebody?" he asked. "I mean — like maybe a witch or something like that."

The idea made Brittany uncomfortable, even though she felt quite sure she no longer had any trouble keeping fairy tales and everyday life very separate. Still, there was something almost hauntingly magical about the house, and even though the lavender-gray twilight now made it seem all the more forlorn, she felt herself drawn toward it in a way she couldn't explain.

"It's almost like the Hansel and Gretel house," Ashley whispered aloud. "The candy one, I mean." Yet she too was puzzled that it wasn't gumdrops or marshmallows or candy canes that seemed to be pulling her like a magnet, but the very run-down, abandoned quality of the ruined cottage.

"We could fix it up," Brittany suggested, trying to be bold.

"Yeah," Tiger chimed in, "and get rid of all those— those old weeds and stuff!"

"But we'll leave the flowers," Ashley said, taking a timid step toward the house.

"Oh yes, we must leave the flowers!" Brittany echoed, looking at the three tall stalks of pink and lavender hollyhocks that rose above the weeds along the front of the cottage.

Quietly, they all moved through the tall grass until they stopped a few feet from the front door. Once painted a deep blue green but now battered and faded, it hung crookedly from a lonely rusted hinge. Through the long, triangular crack you could peer into the gloominess beyond.

"It's too dark in there," Tiger said. "Maybe there's a light to turn on."

Ashley stepped forward and peeked in. In the shadowy interior she could make out the shape of a rickety cot surrounded by broken boxes. Wallpaper hung in strips from the walls and ceiling; junk and bits of plaster littered the floor. Brittany and Tiger craned their necks to see through the narrow opening as Ashley stepped back to survey the doorway.

"Help me," she said, and the three of them scooted the door ajar enough to slip through, Ashley stepping in first, the other two cautiously following.

With a little more light filtering through the larger opening in the doorway, they could see now even the faded flower designs on the tattered wallpaper. And they stared at the sagging cot with its dusty and stained mattress, and the heap of rags and broken chair legs and teacups strewn around the room.

"Are we really going stay here tonight?" Tiger asked softly.

"Tonight," Ashley answered, "and every night." She turned slowly around, her eyes narrowing as she strained to imagine how the interior would look if it were really fixed up.

Brittany swallowed, bothered by the cobwebs in the windows and the bits of broken glass on the dusty floor. Still, she couldn't help feeling a little fountain of excitement beginning to bubble up inside her. "It'll be our home forever," she whispered.

Afraid that the dimming light wouldn't last much longer, the three of them quickly examined the entire cottage. A doorway at one end of the room led into a tinier room scarcely bigger than a large closet. It was darker than the main room and more barren, and one corner contained what looked like a heap of rags but proved to be an old quilt. Back in the main room across from the front door, another doorway revealed a tiny room that might once have been a kitchen; beyond this was still another room where the floor was damp from an opening in the shaggy roof above.

Worried about spiders, Tiger poked with a stick at the various items found in some dusty cardboard boxes:

a rusty water faucet, a musty book with its cover torn off, a chipped teacup, a tarnished doorknob. Ashley started to pry a board from one of the front windows in order to let more light into the room, and Brittany, finding a stiffened broom with two thirds of its handle broken off, began to sweep the clutter of dead leaves, crumbled plaster, and scraps of paper from the warped wooden floor.

Suddenly she squealed: "Look! A fireplace!"

Ashley stopped prying at a slivery board. "I saw it. But how would we light a fire?"

Brittany's spirits sagged. It would have been so perfect, giving them both heat and light. "Oh, I'm *so* cold," she mumbled disappointedly.

"If you're so cold, wear this!" Tiger announced, coming out of the little side room.

"Tiger!" Ashley shrieked. "Put that down! It must be a hundred years old and full of bugs!"

From the end of the stick drooped a mass of soft, rose-colored material trimmed in feathers of the same color.

"What is it?" Brittany asked, touching it with caution.

"I don't know," he answered. "But there's a whole bunch of stuff in a bag in there behind the door."

Brittany picked up one end of the rose-colored cloth while Ashley took the other. As they held it up, they were both startled to see that it was an old-fashioned gown decorated with rose-colored feathers at the neck and the sleeves.

Ashley was aghast. "I can't believe someone wouldn't take this! It's in fabulous condition. I mean, it's old, but—"

"Oh, please," Brittany begged. "Can I put it on? I want to take off these wet clothes so bad."

Ashley felt a twinge of jealousy, but Tiger interrupted her before she could say anything.

"Look! There's lots more!" he said, dragging in a large but tired-looking shopping bag full of old clothes.

Ashley began pulling things out. "Oh, I wish it was lighter in here. I can hardly see anything—!" Suddenly she stopped, her hands touching a soft velvet heap that looked in the twilight as if it might be a deep purple. She held it up and shook it several times to make sure there were no bugs in it. It was a long, full-length robe of some sort, old-fashioned like the pale rose-colored one that Brittany now was pulling over her head. The three of them plunged once more into the wonderful bag and came up with three pairs of ladies' high-heeled shoes to replace their own soggy shoes and socks.

"I'll wear this!" Tiger belted out, holding up a massive wool coat with a fur collar.

"And look what's in the pocket!" he suddenly shrieked, holding out a book of paper matches.

"Matches!" Ashley and Brittany cried out at once. *It's a miracle,* Ashley thought to herself. Matches—just when the cottage was becoming so dark that, within a few more minutes, they would have found themselves in total blackness.

"Hurry!" Brittany urged. "Light a fire!" And the three of them scrambled around the room gathering bits of paper and scraps of wood and cardboard to stack up inside the dusty fireplace. In a matter of seconds the paper ignited, and thick gray smoke, seeming at first as though it were going to pour out into the room, began billowing up the chimney.

"It works!" Tiger cried with delight, tossing a broken chair leg onto the flames. His heavy coat was so long he had to hold it off the ground with one hand.

"Wait a minute!" Ashley cautioned. "Let's not burn anything we might be able to use. We're going to need furniture — and maybe we can find enough broken parts to make a chair — or a table."

"If only my brother Rob were here," Brittany wished out loud. "He could fix anything, I bet." Suddenly she picked up the broken broom and began sweeping vigorously to take her mind off her brother. If only he were here, it would be perfect. After all, he was almost an adult — and it always made you feel better when someone big was around. It was true that he hadn't always treated her very nicely — except for the time when their mother died. They had only known for about three weeks that she was ill: first headaches, then tests at the hospital, and finally the coma she never recovered from. But Rob had been different during that time — talking softer, teasing her less, even offering to take her places. In fact, he had been even more of a father to her than Harold—who was only their stepfather anyway and had never spent much time with them.

It was funny how she didn't really miss Harold—or hadn't felt very sorry when the police took him away. It probably wasn't all his fault—at least not the way her mother had explained it. He had been wounded in the Korean War, long before he had married their mother and before their father had been killed in a car accident, and sometimes Harold's head injuries seemed to make him do strange things. But it was still hard for Brittany to understand words like *embezzlement* and *grand larceny*.

Suddenly she stopped sweeping, struck by how the warm golden glow of the blazing fire behind her seemed to cast a spell over the room. Even things that had looked a little eerie a while ago now seemed to welcome her, as though this truly were going to become "home." The shreds of wallpaper hanging above looked like golden chandeliers; spider webs had become crystal lace.

For another hour they worked on the main room, sorting anything that might possibly be useful from the mass of things that were definitely trash. Before long, two shabby wooden crates and one ragged burlap bag were so stuffed with rubbish they could hardly drag them to the front door to be thrown away when daylight came. The room was filling with shadows again as the last coals sputtered and flickered on the hearth.

"There's nothing more to burn," Ashley announced. "Tomorrow we'll have to gather lots of wood."

Tiger yawned. "When it's light."

Brittany glanced at the stained cot, then at Ashley. "Who—who gets to sleep there?" she asked timidly.

Ashley quickly tried to think. "I know. We'll draw straws." From the broom leaning against the fireplace, she took three straws, tucking them neatly between her thumb and the palm of her hand. "The one who gets the longest straw sleeps on the cot." She took a quick glance at the ends of the straws sticking down in front of her palm, then secretly pulled the longest one down a little further so that it looked like the shortest of all. Brittany stared at her, suspecting a trick; then, noticing how one straw was made to look obviously much shorter than the others, she reached out for it. Ashley tightened her hand and pulled back, and the straw broke.

"*Now* look—" Brittany began to whimper.

But before Ashley could respond, she heard a long sigh from behind them, and they both turned to see Tiger, his closed eyes barely visible above the massive fur collar, curled up on the cot in front of the fire.

Ashley shrugged. "Oh, well. Let him stay there. I'm just glad he went to sleep without crying for something to eat."

Brittany felt a little tug in her empty stomach and wished the Ashley hadn't reminded her that no one had eaten anything since the tuna casserole at school lunch at noon. But she put it out of her mind, her tired legs and aching muscles making her feel as if there was nothing she wanted now more than a long peaceful sleep.

"I know what we can do," Ashley said. "We'll share that quilt in the other room."

With each other for security, the two girls clomped across the room in their high-heels and gowns and slipped into the dark little side room long enough to find the ragged quilt and drag it back in front of the smoldering fire, beside the cot. Together they snuggled — shifting, squirming, and turning for a long time before either of them drifted off to sleep.

As for Tiger, he had fallen into a deep and heavy sleep long ago. And now he dreamed of another time, another cottage, and another set of little people whistling as they worked to make the cottage spic and span. Only it was all mixed up to him. Sometimes he was watching seven dwarves sweeping and dusting and scrubbing, and sometimes he and the girls were helping the dwarves, and sometimes he and Ashley and Brittany were tidying up all by themselves, hurrying to finish before Snow White came home, only it turned out that when she knocked on the door it wasn't Snow White at all but the witch instead and she came right in the cottage and poked at him with her finger and kept cackling in his ear and poking and cackling until suddenly he woke up and —

Tiger sat up with a start. It wasn't a dream. It really

was *not* a dream. When he saw, in the moonlight from the half-boarded window, the old witch poking her finger at him, he screamed louder than he had ever screamed in his life, and the scream echoed and echoed and echoed . . .

# *4*

Tiger's scream was ringing in his own ears, but as the old witch grabbed at him and clapped a bony hand over his mouth, he realized that the echoing shrieks he heard were coming from Ashley and Brittany who were sitting up and shrinking back in horror against the stone fireplace.

"Stop it!" the old witch cried out, her long frizzy hair flying in the moonlight as she threw her head back. "Stop it! Stop it!" She flung out one hand to clutch at the girls. "They'll hear us! Shhh!"

Tiger couldn't believe it. The old woman was holding him now against her breast and rocking back and forth, repeating over and over in her hoarse voice, "Hush, child, hush—or they're going to come and find us!"

Ashley found herself whimpering now, and Brittany's screams had become sobs.

"Oh, please, *please!*" they heard the old crone say. "Don't scream, don't cry, whoever you are. I didn't mean to frighten you."

Tiger tried to pull away, but she continued to clutch him against her as she rocked back and forth.

"Who are you?" she croaked.

"Who are *you?*" asked Ashley. "What are you doing here?"

"What am *I* doing here? I *live* here."

"How *could* you?" shrieked Ashley. "This place was abandoned. We—"

"Shh!" the old lady cautioned, letting Tiger lie back on the cot as she rose up. "We must talk quietly. I'm afraid we've awakened every dog and field mouse in the country," she said. "They mustn't find me, you know!"

"Who mustn't?" Brittany asked. "The dogs and field mice?"

They could see the old lady's tall outline as she stood in the doorway now, looking out. Her hair was silver in the moonlight but her nose and chin were not nearly as pointed as they had all three imagined. Tiger slipped off the cot and snuggled between Ashley and Brittany, his heart still pounding.

"Is she really a witch?" he whispered.

The old lady turned back toward them. "Am I a witch? Did you ask if I'm a witch?" She came toward them. "Are you goblins?" she asked. "Is that what you are?" She gave a little laugh, but her voice seemed shaky as she leaned toward them. "You terrified me, you little devils, do you know that? What are you doing here? Are you all by yourselves?"

Brittany was hoping they could make up something about being on a camping trip and how their parents were just in the next room, but Ashley's voice surprised her as she answered, truthfully, that they were there all alone.

"What have you done to this place?" the witch lady was asking. "You really *are* gnomes, aren't you? Elves that come with mischief and magic and switch everything around—" Suddenly she struck a match, and the three children shrank back, startled.

"Did you really do this all by yourselves?" the woman asked, looking around her at the freshly swept floor and the boxes of rubbish piled neatly by the doorway. They stared at her, her face illuminated by the yellow glow from the match she held. If she wasn't a witch, what was she? She had on a strange rust-colored dress that looked wrinkled but not dirty. And though her lined face was definitely old, there was something so young about her eyes—something so haunting and beautiful—that it made the children almost shiver. Tiger felt as if he wanted to ask her if she were Glinda, the good witch of the North, but then the match went out.

She quickly struck another one, and they found she was looking at them.

"Well—" she said softly and slowly, her eyes passing from one to the other. She sat down on the edge of the cot while the children continued to huddle together in front of the dark hole that was the fireplace.

"Imagine that . . . " she went on, peering at them so intently that they felt cold chills. "What pretty little bodies to be hiding such terrifying and devilish little gnomes who come in the night and fill my life with such earth-quakes and whirlwinds . . . "

"*What* did we do?" Tiger asked, puzzled, looking at Ashley.

Ashley ignored him. "Do—do you really live here?" she asked the witch-lady, feeling a heavy disappointment taking over her body. It would mean that the cottage could never be theirs, that they could never fix it up the way they had dreamed just a few hours before.

The match was burning low and the lady shook it out, still not answering Ashley's question.

"Why don't you light a fire?" Brittany timidly suggested.

"Oh, I wouldn't do that," they heard her say. "Someone might see the light and know we're in here."

"But *we* made a fire," Tiger spoke up.

"Well, not a very big one," Ashley put in quickly. She looked around at the two partially covered windows in the room and the crooked door that didn't quite cover the doorway. "But if we covered up the windows—and propped the door back in place—maybe we could make a fire and no one would know."

The lady struck another match and now held it out towards Ashley's face as she studied her. "What a clever little elf-child you are. All of you," she added, looking at Tiger and Brittany as well. "Clever and brave."

She rose up. "I have part of a candle somewhere—if I can only find it." She disappeared, with her match, into the little room at the end, but they could still hear her mumbling: "I *did* have a candle. But little night fairies have rearranged everything—and even stolen my quilt—and my clothes."

In the dark, the children gasped and nudged one another uncomfortably.

"This is *her* coat?" Tiger whispered nervously.

Brittany tugged at the sleeve of Ashley's gown and whispered: "What I don't get is—if this is her house, why is she so afraid someone will know she's here?"

"Ah hah," they heard a voice say, and they saw the lady step into the path of moonlight as she came across the room toward them. "You're whispering," she said. "You must think I'm as deaf as an old doorknob, but I'm not. Oh no, not at all." She lit a stub of a candle and went on: "These ears, these eyes—they miss nothing. Nothing! Do you understand that?" Then she mumbled: "No, no, I can't afford to let them miss a thing. Life is too short—too short for that!"

She propped the candle on one of the rough stones along the top of the fireplace where the mantle should have been. It gave the room a kind of eerie light and cast a large shadow behind her that stretched across the room and partway up the wall. Then she sat down on the cot in front of them.

"Little thieves," she said, her eyes narrowing as she looked at them. "What do I do with three little thieves?"

Tiger felt almost as though he were shrinking. He

wanted to pull the big coat off and give it to her, but the thought that he was naked underneath made him whimper out loud as he nestled in closer between Ashley and Brittany.

"Do you know that that gown you're wearing is Viennese?" she asked, and Brittany shrunk back, feeling the lady's eyes directly on her. *Viennese,* she thought. What did that mean?

"I bought that in Vienna in 1912," the lady said, pronouncing every word slowly and carefully. "No, I didn't either. It was given to me. By a Rumanian count." She leaned in closely, just inches away from their faces. "And you would never believe what it cost." She paused. "Hundreds of dollars. And you were *sleeping* in it — on the floor."

Brittany squeezed her eyes tight, trying not to make a sound, but she could feel the tears building up.

"Well, we won't cry about that, will we?" the lady said, straightening up. "I shouldn't have left it here where just anyone could find it. Thank heavens I hid all my jewels."

Brittany opened her eyes and stared at her.

"Are you a queen — or what?" Tiger whispered.

"Ah hah," the lady said. "You're clever — and you're quick. You know royalty, don't you?"

The children all exchanged quick glances and then stared at her.

"Have you ever heard of Anastasia?" she whispered

to them. "The Russian princess who escaped when the Czar was executed in 1918?"

They all shook their heads, although Ashley wished with all heart that she *had* heard about it.

"Is that you?" Brittany whispered.

The old lady paused, and her eyes grew soft. "I'm not really sure, unfortunately," she said, and her voice sounded lonely and quiet. "I could tell you, 'Yes, I'm Anastasia,' but I want to tell you the truth: I don't really know." Her voice grew to be only a whisper. "I've got royal blood—I'm quite certain of that. And I'm almost exactly the right age. And I've *played* Anastasia—that is, I've played the Empress, her grandmother, in the play." She paused. "I'm an actress, you see. And a rather famous one, too."

"Have you ever played the part of Glinda?" Tiger asked.

The lady smiled but shook her head.

"Have—have we heard of you?" Ashley dared to ask.

"Oh, my goodness—you must have," the lady said. "How old are you little creatures? Twenty-five? Thirty? You do go to college, don't you?"

Tiger almost giggled, but he still felt so nervous that the sound never came out.

"Still too young," she said. "But your parents and your grandparents—they would have known me. I was known *par tout*—that means *everywhere*, in French," she put in. "In the twenties and thirties I played all the major theaters and concert halls in Europe." She bent in closer again. "They loved me. You'll find me in their dusty old albums — among the pressed roses and souvenir programs," she whispered.

Ashley stared at her, and next to the hungry feeling in the pit of her stomach, she felt a strange ache — a longing to search through all the albums and scrapbooks in the world to find the pictures — much younger and much prettier — of this strange lady with the long gray hair who sat before them.

"What were you called?" Ashley asked.

The lady hesitated. "I was called then exactly what I'm called today. Cassandra. Cassandra du Maurier." Then she leaned in and added quickly: "But you may call me Cassie."

"Cassie," Tiger pronounced softly.

"You *will* stay with me a while, won't you? How long can you stay?"

Both Tiger and Brittany looked at Ashley, who swallowed and then announced bravely: "We could probably stay for a while. If it's all right with you."

"Well, I'd be silly to let you go, wouldn't I? I'm not saying that I don't have talent — even possibly a few magic powers. But you performed a trick with this funny little house that even Houdini couldn't have accomplished. I suppose you know *he* was a very famous magician," she added.

"What was our trick?" Tiger whispered to the girls.

"Why, *this!*" Cassandra du Maurier said, holding her arms out to indicate the tidy floor and the bulging boxes and burlap bag arranged neatly against the wall.

"We had really just gotten started," Ashley said boldly. "We had plans to do so much more!"

"Well, then I must keep you here with me, mustn't I?"

"We didn't even dream anyone lived here — " Brittany started to say.

"Oh, they don't. I mean, they *didn't*," Cassie said. "I've been here only three or four days. That was my bed in there," she said, indicating the little room down at the end. "When I came back in the middle of the night — I had to walk all the way here, you see — I just knew something was wrong. The door seemed to have been moved a little — and nothing crunched under my feet when I crept across the floor to *ma petite chambre.* That's French, you know — for *my little chamber.* I had made me a little bed on the floor there, you see. But when I got there and crept around on my hands and knees, I couldn't find my quilt — or any of my things. And then the moon came out from behind a cloud, and I saw you all spread out here in front of the fireplace." She paused, looking at them sideways. "You haven't told me what you're doing here. How do I know you're not spies? Where are your parents?"

Ashley opened her mouth to speak but nothing came out.

"You're running away, aren't you? You hate your violin lessons and you hate brussels sprouts and you're all running away."

Brittany swallowed and nodded, even though it wasn't quite right.

"Well, then we'll get along just marvelously, won't we?" Cassie rose up and, with one puff, blew out the candle. Neither Ashley nor Brittany nor Tiger breathed as they waited, still huddled on the floor, while Cassandra du Maurier seemed to be fumbling with the ragged quilt in front of them. Then they felt her push them gently down and squeeze in beside them, pulling the quilt up over them all.

"If you're going to grow up to be beautiful like me," she said, "you girls simply must get your beauty sleep. And that includes you too, little prince—or you might get freckles and warts. I don't keep a clock—but I'm certain it must be centuries past midnight."

They lay still, almost afraid to take a breath, as they felt her squirm and wriggle for a moment between them. To Brittany she smelled like cinnamon and apples and old books.

All was quiet for a moment, then she said: "We're all in this together, you know. Even now, on the news, some sleepy old announcer somewhere must be mumbling to the world about three runaway midgets. You *are* midgets, aren't you? You're much too brilliant and witty and clever to be mere children." She sighed. "I've been gone for nearly a week, I think, but I doubt if anyone has even missed *me* yet. But you three runaways — you will surely make the news."

Three runaways. Ashley tried to picture, in her mind, how it might look in the papers or sound on the TV. Three runaways.

As if she had read her mind, Cassie du Marrier sighed once more and said aloud, happily but softly: "That makes four of us now, you see."

A streak of light fell across Ashley's face, and she sat up quickly, blinking. The soft daylight not only crept into the room through the windows, but now, while the crooked front door was being pushed aside and scraping across the crumbling doorstep, a wide path of light fell into the room.

Ashley blinked again, trying to put together in her mind the strange events of the night before and remembering that the gray-haired lady almost floating through the doorway was Cassandra du Maurier. Ashley stared in wonderment as the woman, a large bouquet of flowers in one hand and her long silky green skirt in the other, swooped through the doorway. No wonder Tiger had envisioned her as Glinda, the good witch of the North!

*"Bonjour! Buon Giorno! Dobry dyen!"* She chirped vigorously. "I've been playing games with the sun. Hide-and-seek!" She bent down towards Ashley and her voice grew softer. "Something woke me up just when the sky was beginning to get cantaloupe-colored, and I decided to hurry out and gather some flowers while it was still as dark as a whisper. But I had to move quickly because the sun kept peeking over the hill like a big ripe peach

and I knew that, if it caught me too far out into the fields, my little game would be over ... "

"What game?" Tiger asked, sitting up. Brittany too stirred beside him.

"Why, making ourselves invisible!" Cassie exclaimed, smiling at them. Her long ripply gray hair still hung down past her shoulders, but in the daylight now she no longer seemed like a witch but a fairy godmother.

For a second she looked at the three open-mouthed children, then, giving her long green dress a final swoosh in a little half-whirl, she picked three wild daisies from her bouquet and stuck them in her hair.

"There!" she announced. "How's that? If we can't make ourselves quite as invisible as we'd wish, then we'll simply blend with the grass and the flowers." She hesitated. "Of course, you realize that's why I wore my new-mown-hay dress!" Before they could answer, she picked up once again the long circular skirt of her dress, and whirled around twice.

"You look like a bride," Tiger mumbled. And she did—bouquet and all.

"Well, bless your heart!" replied Cassie, her eyes sparkling. "We won't worry that my grassy-green dress is a little wrinkled, will we? It's been packed in a paper bag," she whispered. "But you're exactly right, little prince. Today I guess I *am* a bride—a *beautiful* bride—for I've just married the spirit of the morning and vowed with all my heart to be loyal and faithful and true—"

"Clear until noon!" Brittany squealed, almost surprising herself with her own voice.

"Until noon?" Cassie asked, looking puzzled.

"And then you'll have to get a divorce and marry the afternoon!" Brittany tried to explain.

"Oh, my, no! Oh, no, no, no, my little love! Oh no, I'm much too loyal for that. When I marry, dear, it's for always! Till death do us—no, not even then!"

She leaned down toward them and tried to turn her bright expression into a threatening frown. "You haven't been doing your homework, have you?" She asked, shaking a long finger at them. "You haven't been reading your Thoreau." She straightened up. "And how would poor Henry David feel if *he* knew that?"

"Who's Henry?" Tiger wanted to know.

"Who's *Henry?*" Cassie exclaimed. "Oh!" she went on, putting her hands, and even the bouquet, to her breast. "Imagine that! Three little pygmies who don't even know Henry David Thoreau! Well! We can't let another second go by without introductions, can we?"

She bent over in a kind of exaggerated curtsy, motioning first to an invisible figure beside her, and then to the children. "Sir Henry, the children. Children, Sir Henry!" Then she paused, looking puzzled. "Why, how positively embarrassing. I don't even know your names!"

Tiger opened his mouth to inform her but stopped when Cassie suddenly thrust out her palm, almost like the road-guard at school. "Stop!" she said, studying their faces carefully. "Let me guess. Surely not everyday names like Mary and Susan and Tom. Or John and Betty and Alice. Could it be Periwinkle or Paddywiskit or Pittleweeps? How about Peppermint? or Crystal? Ah — that's my favorite!" And she said it again — "Crystal" — this time softer, making the syllables shimmer and glisten as they slipped through her lips.

"I'm Tiger!" Ashley heard her brother announce boldly. "But my name's really Theodore — if that sounds better."

"Tiger! Theodore! Oh my!" cried Cassie. "How can we choose? They're both *music!* I think I might have to call you Tigedore in order to use them both!" Then she looked at him sideways. "I thought I was going to call you Wriggletto after last night — the way you wriggled and squiggled until I finally couldn't sleep another wink and had to get up, before dawn, and go gathering flowers!" She looked at her bouquet and pulled out some little yellow flowers that she stuck in Tiger's tousled hair. "Oh, well, we won't worry about that, will we? At least I did all my flower-gathering before even the sun got a good peep at me!" She looked at Brittany. "If *he's* Tiger, my dear — who are you? Dragonfly? Hummingbird? Water Sprite?"

"Brittany," she said timidly.

"Oh, my!" Cassie responded, her hands going once more to her breast. Then she plucked from her bouquet several tiny blue and lavender flowers that she carefully placed among Brittany's dark curls. "Brittany," she said over and over. "It's too beautiful to be a real name. It smells like the seacoast and has the faraway chirp of sea gulls in it."

Tiger giggled, and Cassie reached out and touched Brittany's cheek for a moment before she turned from her to look at Ashley.

"I don't know if I can bear another beautiful name— all in the very same morning," she said. "But—try me."

Ashley hesitated for a second, then breathed out her own name as magically as she could: "Ashley."

"Oooooh!" Cassie shrieked, her voice almost like someone running their fingers across the strings of a harp. "Stop it, stop it, *please!* I really am mortal, in spite of what you might think—! And we fragile mortal beings can only stand so much stardust and moonbeams! Oh, my! Ashhhhhhley," she said, closing her eyes and weaving her head back and forth as she seemed to savor it. "Too much, too much," she breathed, holding up one shaking palm.

"Really?" Ashley said, with disappointment. "Too much?"

Cassie partly opened her eyes and stared at Ashley sideways. "Well . . . no, perhaps not—as long as we just whisper it. It's quite exquisite, you know, like crystal, and we wouldn't want to shatter it into thousands of little sparkling pieces. Just keep it a whisper," she said, "and I think I can bear it."

The children exchanged excited glances with each other.

"Cassandra's the most beautiful name of all," Brittany said.

"Oh, please," Cassie said, again holding up the palm of her hand. "Don't even mention it. Someone very lovely and very pretty had that name once."

"Who?" Tiger asked.

"Why *me*, of course!" she tittered and began quickly choosing all the deep and pale pink flowers to arrange in Ashley's long honey-colored hair.

"You've got the colors backwards," Tiger snickered. "Britttany's got on the pink dress and Ashley's—"

"Oh, no, no, little prince. *They've* got them backwards. Ashley is the daughter of apple blossoms, of strawberries and pomegranates and pink lemonade. Just look at her and you can see it—and Brittany is the bluebell and the bob-o-link and—"

"Aren't bob-o-links sort of grayish brown?" Ashley asked.

"Don't quibble, dear. You're quibbling—and that means you're finding fault. No, no matter what its color, the bob-o-link's *name* is blue, and that's all that matters." She stopped for a moment, studying the wrinkled gowns the girls were wearing. "Yes, you really must switch, I suppose. Although I think I remember bringing those elegant gowns for *me*—in case I need to perform—or go to a ball—or who knows? Well, we'll really have to decide what we're going to do about your clothes—"

"Maybe our real clothes might be dry now—" Brittany began, meekly.

"No, no, no, no," Cassie said with an elaborate wave of her hand, "that would be much too ordinary. If this time here in the woods is to be an extraordinary experience, then, of course, we must dress extraordinarily!" She beamed at Tiger as if seeking his approval, and when he smiled back, she went on: "If you're going to go out into the world—in broad daylight—then we might have to camouflage you—perhaps like butterflies or whippoorwills. But we'll worry about that a little later. First I have to find my poor little birds something to eat!"

"But don't we get to meet Henry?" Tiger asked.

"Henry? Oh, my, yes—poor Henry David!" Cassie said, embarrassed. "We've left him standing here in his frock coat, hat in hand, waiting all this time when he *could* have been out examining birds' nests or finches' wings."

Tiger looked around the cottage, half-expecting to see someone waiting there. "Dear Henry David—these are the children," Cassie announced. "We shan't say their names again for fear we'll all wither and shrivel at the very tinkle of those delicate little melodies!" Turning from her imaginary friend, she addressed the children: "Henry David Thoreau was a most marvelous human being who lived a hundred and fifty years ago and wrote some very beautiful things about life and nature and people. We must read all about that sometime. But where was I? Why did we even try to fetch him here in the first place? What were we talking about?"

"About your marriage!" cried Brittany.

"To the spirit of the morning!" Tiger added.

"Ah, yes," Cassie said, and her eyes grew soft and sparkly. "The *morning*. Well, you see, I got up quickly when I saw the darkness disappearing like old smoke and the sun hiding behind a hill but getting ready to set the world on fire all over again, and I slipped on this dress from my bag there so I could be part of the meadows and trees and the willows and the grass. And I ran through the fields and along the river—"

"There's a river?" Tiger interrupted.

"Oh, yes, love—a winding little stream hiding in the trees that will even talk to you if you'll take the time to listen."

"It *will?*" he asked.

"It knows all the languages—although I haven't tried Arabic yet. That's one we'll try together one time. But as I scurried through the fields and the trees, playing my little hide-and-seek with that sneaky old sun, picking Queen Anne's lace here, gathering goldenrod there, I learned all over again something I think I've known forever."

"What's that?" asked Ashley.

"That what dear Henry David once said is *so* true: morning is the most memorable season of the day, the awakening hour. That's the time when we're most alert to sounds, to smells, to tastes—to the world around us. There is something awake in us then that sleeps all the rest of the day—and when we're most awake, then, of course, that's when we're most alive. We must always remember to listen to the morning inside of us."

"In me, too?" Tiger asked.

"Oh, little Tigedore! You are so *full* of the morning that I expect any minute to see it tumbling out of your ears and spilling out of—"

"Can you *feel* it?" Brittany asked Ashley, anxiously. "I think maybe *I* do."

"Mainly I'm feeling hungry," Ashley murmured.

"Then *come!*" Cassie urged. "Let me make sure there's no one about, and we'll sneak out through the tall grass like petals blown by the wind until we come to a little place by the brook so enchanted that I think we could eat dandelions and cockleburs and swear it was the most delicious breakfast ever!"

"Really?" Tiger asked, wide-eyed.

"Would I tell you anything that wasn't true?" Cassie replied in amazement. And with that she tossed the remaining wildflowers in the air so they fell in a shower of color around them, swooped up her long green dress, and swirled toward the open doorway, the three children bounding after her.

Holding up the long gowns and teetering on their high heels, the two girls stepped through the doorway, Tiger stumbling behind.

"Do I still have to wear these shoes — and this coat?" he asked.

"Shh!" Cassie cautioned, looking both ways as she stepped down from the crumbling doorstep surrounded by hollyhocks and out into the tall green grass. Then she whispered quickly: "Go peek in one of those bags I brought back last night. You'll find a big woolly sweater you can wear. And don't worry about shoes — we'll go barefoot, you and I!"

"Do *I* have to go barefoot, too?" Brittany asked.

Ashley, too, hesitated on the edge of the tall grass, tempted to leave the awkward borrowed shoes behind in order to let her feet feel the grass's cool freshness, yet fearing at the same time that she might step on a thorn or, worse still, a squashy worm or even a lizard.

"Well," said Cassie, "certainly no one *has* to go barefoot — if they want to miss the fresh cool grass between their toes. As for myself, I simply relish the feel of the damp greenness on the soles of my feet, reminding me it's now May—and not February or March. But," she said, surveying the girls' feet, "if you want to keep a good safe distance between you and springtime, just stay in those shoes. But just make sure," she added, "that you don't turn your ankle and break the heels off. I may need to wear one of those pair next time I'm invited to a concert or a ball."

Tiger returned, pulling a lumpy oatmeal-colored sweater down over his head, knocking one of the yellow flowers from his hair. The sweater came down below his knees, and he had to pull the sleeves up on his arms. "Oh well," he said, "at least it's dry. My pants and shirt are still soaked. And, anyway, they do look sort of— ordinary."

Ashley looked at Tiger's bare feet, then Cassie's. Suddenly she stepped out of the high heels, letting each foot step down off the doorstep onto the cool damp grass. Brittany, too, hesitated only a second before she hitched up the long rose-colored gown with the feathers, shook off her shoes, and followed behind them.

"We're in a marvelous spot, you see," Cassie called back over her shoulder. "Absolutely perfect! There's not a soul around to spy on us. We're oodles of footsteps always from the nearest farmhouse, and we're snuggled away here, hidden from the main road by that wonderful little patch of woods. The fields out this way," she said, turning and motioning back to them, "seem as forgotten as our little house. That's why the road's all smothered in weeds. Poor little road—perhaps it never wandered much further than our little cottage here, anyway. But how positively lucky we are that it dead-ends right there where it does! That means, you see, that no one in the world would ever have any possible reason to come scooting by—unless they purposely had their mind set on coming directly to our little place."

"But who owns it?" Ashley asked. "The cottage, I mean."

"Goodness, child, who knows? A family of hedgehogs? A troll? There *is* a rumor," Cassie said, her voice becoming a mysterious whisper, "that it's presently occupied by three runaway dwarves and a strange enchantress of some kind—but we certainly can't believe rumors, can we?"

"Three runaway dwarves," Tiger pondered, stepping through the high grass. "Do you mean *us?*"

"Ssh!" Cassie winked. "The trees have ears." And as she led them off into the little thicket where vines drooped down from branches overhead, they could hear the first faint gurgling sound of the brook. The early morning light sifted down through the leaves to where flowers of soft lavender and dusty rose grew among the greenery.

"Look!" Cassie called, keeping her voice low as though afraid to break the hush that seemed to hang over the little grove. "There are berries here—and they're

positively scrumptious! I tried them day before yesterday."

"Mmmmm! They're good!" Brittany said, tasting one
of the deep-red berries. "Is this what we're going to live
on?"

"Well," Cassie said, "they'll help. Pretend they're
apricots or pork sausages or blueberry muffins — whatever you're hungry for. I'm afraid our cupboard is a little
bare — until we can put our heads together and come up
with some menus that will dazzle even the most experienced *gourmet!* That's someone who has tasted all the
most exquisite dishes the world can offer!" she added.

"But how —?" Brittany wanted to know. "You mean
we're going to pretend that — "

"Oh, no!" Cassie cut in quickly. "I mean, yes — imagination certainly needs to be a part of it! Why, with a little
sage and a dash of curry, I can travel all the way to Bombay
or Kashmir on a hamburger. But, no, no, dear love, we
can't be quite that exotic yet — not without a single spice
to our name. But I have an idea. Pick some more berries
and then I'll tell you all about it."

She began busily plucking at the dark plump berries
hidden among the green leaves, and Brittany and Ashley
followed her. When they reached a grassy spot near the
edge of the stream, she plopped herself down and motioned to the others to do the same.

"I scurried into town late yesterday afternoon, you
see — mainly to get some more things, like clothes and

dishes and a pan or two. Perhaps you peeked at them in the three large bags of things I brought back with me last night."

The children shook their heads as she went on almost talking to herself. "What a pity I didn't know at the time that there would be four of us! But anyway—"

"Where did you get the things?" Ashley cut in. "Do you have a house there? In Chesterton?"

"Oh, no, my dear! Certainly not! I mean, I have con- tacts there—a relative or two—which I am taking care to avoid at this time," she murmured half under her breath. "Poor dears," she went on. "They know nothing about acting, about the theater, about nature, about magic—! No, no," she sighed. "*My* home, you see, is a most elegant Victorian mansion—an *estate,* my child— miles and miles and miles from here. It's just that, I'm *here*—and making do with what I can—for now, you un- derstand. Just a little spree, you might call it—getting back in touch with nature—rediscovering the *morning* in me—and listening very carefully to what it tells me."

Not taking their eyes from her, the three hungry children continued to poke berries into their mouths, savoring every juicy-sweet bite as they clung to each word that Cassie spoke.

"We must have just missed you, then!" Ashley cut in. "It was only about a half hour after the rain let up when we stumbled onto the cottage!"

"Well, what a lucky thing it was we didn't see each

other! I'm afraid if I had seen you coming I might have shrunk and withered and shriveled into nothing more than an old weed by the side of the road. Does that surprise you, coming from someone who spent most of her life behind the footlights—performing before thousands—on the great stages of the world? But, I must admit, I'm really quite allergic to people right now—that is, *ordinary* people. But how could I ever have known that *you* would be so *extra*ordinary?"

Both Ashley and Brittany expected Tiger to exclaim: "We *are?*" but he only grinned and blushed, scrunching up his shoulders until his neck disappeared down into the sweater.

Cassie nibbled delicately on a berry as though she wanted to prolong the flavor as long as possible, then she went on: "Anyway—on my way, I came across the most amazing thing. It was an animal."

Tiger looked puzzled. "Do you mean—like a dragon or something?" Suddenly he felt embarrassed for having said it. Of course he didn't believe in things like that. It was just that everything since last night had become so unreal that he wasn't sure anymore quite what he could really count on as real.

"Oh, nothing as ordinary as all that!" Cassie cried. "No—it was something fantastic and strange and marvelous. It was a cow."

For a second the children were struck dumb. Then

Tiger decided he hadn't heard right. "It was a what?" he asked.

"A cow! Can you believe it?"

Ashley and Brittany looked at each other.

"I'm not making it up at all," Cassie continued. "Cross my heart: it was a cow."

Not knowing what to say, Ashley fumbled for words: "Do you mean—in the field?"

"Ooooh!" Cassie shrieked. "You guessed it. Right in *our* fields—not far from the cottage."

*Well, imagine that!* Ashley wanted to say, sarcastically; but something contagious in the wonder and excitement of Cassie's voice made her stop.

"Do you mean—like a purple cow or something like that?" Tiger wanted to know.

"Oh, no, little prince! More wonderful than that! Can you believe? It was pure white—with black spots." Cassie's eyes widened and stayed that way for a moment while she paused. "That cow," she went on, looking at the children intently, "will save us."

"It will?" Brittany asked, realizing at the same time that she sounded very much like Tiger.

"Oh, absolutely!" Cassie said. "I checked."

They all three looked at her.

"It's not the *only* cow, you see. There were others— and they all had bags just ready to burst—with fresh, warm milk. But it was this certain cow—our cow—that I talked to, as I climbed under the fence and cut across the field. 'Cow,' I said—for that's her name—'Cow, we need to have a rendezvous—an appointment.' And I told her I couldn't stop just then, but that I was going into the town and I would somehow find a bucket or a pan or even a little cup—but I would be coming back. And, you know what? I found a most perfect little pail while I was rummaging around at the church and—"

"At the church? What church?" Ashley wanted to know.

"Well," Cassie started, "I did need some more things, like I said—and so I slipped into town just after dark. I got a ride, you see, in the back of a pick-up truck. Anyway, I marched directly to the church near by the place where I stayed for a while once upon a time. I was hoping that the back door to the church wouldn't be locked, and it wasn't—because the custodian was rumbling around somewhere in the building."

"You mean you stole all those things?" Ashley asked.

"*Stole,* my dear?" asked Cassie, as though she were unable to believe her ears. "Well! That's hardly what I would have called it—although I suppose I stole them just the way three little gnomes stole my quilt last night—as well as those fancy clothes you're wearing this very minute, my love."

"We only borrowed them—" Ashley started to say.

"Oh—*borrow,* is it? Well, then, that's exactly what *I* did. These clothes, you see, mostly belong to me. Oh, it's true—but it's a terribly long story—and positively full of so many adventures and catastrophes and narrow escapes — that I can't possibly tell you now, but — "

"Oh, please tell us!" Brittany begged.

"No, no, no — there'll be sunny afternoons enough for that. Just trust me now, dear chipmunks, to tell you that I had taken much of my beautiful wardrobe and donated it to the church. After all, I had so much — not only incredibly lavish costumes from my theater wardrobe, but gowns from Paris, scarves and ribbons from Hungary and Czechoslovakia — so much really that I simply gave many of them up for costumes and rummage sales and — whatever! But once I decided to completely run away, I suddenly found myself out here in the woods with just a valise or two of — "

"What's a valise?" Tiger broke in

"A suitcase," Ashley responded, hushing him.

"Do you mean the shopping bag where we found these gowns?" Brittany asked, holding up a corner of the long rose dress she was wearing.

"Well," began Cassie, "yes — more or less. All my elegant luggage is at the estate. Some of my most beautiful bags, of course, were stolen in Albania and Madagascar and who knows where else. But one must make do. Life does go on, doesn't it? Anyway to make a long, long story so very, very, very short, just let me confide to you, in absolute secrecy, that I slipped up the stairs and into the attic of that church where everything is stored and took back a few of my most precious things —

plus a dish or two — and, of course, this wonderful little pail we'll use when we go this evening to keep our rendezvous with Cow."

"I don't get it," Tiger said. "Do you mean we're going to drink *cow's* milk?"

"Real cow's milk!" Cassie told him. "Wave good-bye forever to waxy cardboard boxes and plastic containers — we've got a date with a real cow!"

"But is real cow milk as good as plastic milk?" Tiger asked.

Brittany giggled and Ashley rolled her eyes, but Cassie touched Tiger lightly on the cheek.

"Dear little prince, I'll let *you* tell me how good it is — when we pour rich thick cream over tomorrow's ripe berries and when we make delicious puddings and fresh creamy yogurt. Of course, you all know how to cook — ?" she asked, looking carefully at Ashley and Brittany.

"Well — " Ashley began, remembering that the Oglethorpes' kitchen had been off limits except for the times she had had to cut up turnips or peel potatoes.

"Never mind," Cassie chirped, holding up her hands. "That's perfectly all right — because we're going to be fixing such exotic and delicious tidbits that anything found in a mere recipe book will seem positively humdrum and commonplace indeed!"

For the next two hours they picked berries, waded

in the stream, picked more berries, then experimented with making musical instruments out of folded leaves and hollow reeds. They left no inch of the woods unexamined, surprising a chipmunk here, spying quietly on a woodpecker there.

Exhausted, Ashley plopped down by a tree, watching Cassie as she flitted about naming the wildflowers for Tiger and Brittany. Were they really going to become a household, the four of them?

Her mind wandered, uneasily, to the Oglethorpes. What would they be doing this minute? Had the four children gone to school as usual — or had the whole family stayed home to search the neighborhood for their three missing foster children? Mr. Oglethorpe was probably glad they were gone; he always seemed to find them a bother anyway. But Mrs. Oglethorpe would probably worry a little — mainly because now they would have to give up the monthly assistance check unless they could get the children back.

She thought about her real mother, too, and how long it had been since she had seen her. She really did feel sorry for her — the way she would drink because she was sad, and then, when it turned out to make her sadder than ever, how she would break things and cry and lock herself in her room. There had been times, Ashley remembered, when she had wanted to be with her mother, when she had wanted the three of them — she, her mother, and Tiger — to move somewhere nice and be

happy forever. But it had never turned out that way—
and once, when her mother had started screaming and
beating Tiger, Ashley had had to pull him away from her
and hide him under the stairs where the two of them had
finally sobbed themselves to sleep. She had realized then
that her mother didn't really want to be a mother at all
and that it was better, for all of them, if she and Tiger
lived somewhere else.

But now—and she felt her face breaking into a relieved smile just to think of it—now things might not only
be better than at the Oglethorpes, they could be perfect!
*If only it will last,* she said to herself over and over, squeezing her eyes shut and crossing her fingers so tightly they
hurt.

Something suddenly blocked the morning sun, throwing a long cool shadow over where she sat. Looking up
with a gasp, she saw a tall silhouetted figure looming
above her.

For a moment Ashley's heart sank. Then the figure towering over her shifted, and she heard Cassie's soothing voice saying, "You're as white as a snowflake! I didn't mean to turn you into a ghost!"

"*You're* the ghost!" Ashley replied. "I didn't hear you coming at all!"

"I flew!" Cassie whispered. Then she smiled. "At least I try to float, walking as softly as I can." She looked around her. "The noise, you know. I wouldn't want to frighten away the butterflies or terrify a squirrel. Besides, it's a good habit to get into, teetering, as we are, on the edge of the real world."

Ashley sat up, knowing what Cassie meant. She looked off through the trees, picturing in her mind the fields, the farmhouses, and the main road beyond.

"Oh, Cassie—do you think they're going to find us?"

"Oh, my lovely—don't worry your pretty head with such thoughts. Life is too precious, too short. Let's simply love each minute we have here. And if we'll only remember to keep a few rules—"

"Rules?" Ashley asked, cutting her off.

"Oh, they're dreadful little things, rules are—like hornets and ants. But I'm afraid they're part of life—and we have to keep them. One rule: no fires until after dark; the smoke, you see, would positively give us away. That means no cooking for breakfast or lunch—unless we get up before it's light. Another rule: cover our windows, when we light up the cottage at night. Another—"

Her words were broken off as Brittany ran toward them, holding up the little white pail. "I emptied all the berries," she cried, "and rinsed it out in the stream like you said!"

"Brittany!" Ashley scolded in a harsh whisper. "Don't be so loud!"

Cassie threw her arm around Brittany, pulling her close. "No cross words," she cautioned Ashley. "I'm certain no one heard a single peep—and if they did, they would have thought it was simply that—a peep. My little Brittany has a voice like a *petit oiseau*. That's French," she explained, "for *little bird.*"

"I just don't want anyone to hear us—" Ashley began.

"As long as we're cheerful as birds—and dress like the flowers, we'll all be quite invisible, I promise. Right now," Cassie went on, smiling as Tiger approached with a bouquet of flowers, "we ought to try our hands at another magic trick: transforming that little home of ours into something truly wonderful!"

"Really?" Tiger asked.

"Most certainly! If we hurry now, while we're so full of morning, who know what wonders we might perform?"

Her warm eyes flitted over the three of them, then settled for a moment on Tiger. "Are you ready, little prince?"

"Ready!" he bounced back.

When they arrived at the cottage, their arms filled with ferns and wildflowers, they went to work immediately, cleaning and sweeping and scrubbing every room. And as the last boards covering the windows were finally pried loose, any shadows left inside were chased away by the warm sunny light.

"Now can I put the flowers up?" Tiger kept asking. He had found several empty and dusty bottles of various shapes and sizes, and after rinsing them in the stream, had filled them with the flowers they had picked.

"Not yet," the others kept reminding him, always finding one more spot that needed dusting, scraping, patching, or polishing. While Cassie hauled the trash out into the trees and buried it, Ashley scrubbed at the warped floors with water from the stream and bits of old rags, and Brittany cleaned the windowpanes and carefully tore off the tattered edges of the wallpaper that had been dangling down. It was Tiger's job to gather up pieces of wood that might be useful and to stack them in two neat piles.

"Remember," Cassie cautioned. "We must keep some scraps of wood for the fireplace. And whatever bits of wood might fit tidily into the windows we'll keep so that we can always cover them up and block out the light whenever we are about to light a candle or start a fire."

"What will happen when our candle finally burns down?" Brittany spoke up. "It was teeny enough last night."

"I must remember to try to magic another one when I go into town," Cassie said.

"When we do need the candle—or when we have to have a fire," Ashley put in, "what if we had curtains, heavy thick ones, that we could pull to keep the light from being seen through the trees?"

"Brilliant!" Cassie said. "I'll jot it down on my list of things we need and see what I can come up with."

"But wouldn't we still have to prop up boards in the windows anyway?" Brittany asked. "So that the house will look abandoned from the outside in case anyone happens to come by?"

"What deliciously clever children you are! You don't miss anything, do you? Here's an idea. Just to make sure that no one tries driving down this old overgrown road looking for a place to turn around after a Sunday afternoon drive, let's see if we can find something—maybe an old log—that we could drag across the road to block it!"

"Great plan!" Brittany exclaimed. "Cassie, you have the best ideas in the world!"

"Oh!" she squealed. "You're just saying that. But say it again anyway—a dozen times!"

It didn't take long to find a dead tree lying in the

weeds and tall grass at the edge of the woods. It took longer, however, for them to move it, but after many grunts and sighs, the four of them rallied together at the small end and, lifting it almost shoulder high, were able to drag it through the grass and twigs until it rested diagonally across the abandoned road.

"There!" Cassie beamed, sitting down on the mossy log and dusting off her hands against one another. "That should block us off completely from the whole outside world."

Ashley looked at her and almost wanted to hug her. Still dressed in her long green gown, her gray hair still rippling down below her shoulders, she seemed both old and young at the same time. Ashley watched her as she bent down and helped Tiger remove a sliver from his thumb. Where did she come from, this grandmother-child? From another century? From another world altogether? A realm inhabited by spirits and fairy folk?

As if she read her mind, Cassie stood up and smiled at Ashley. "How pretty you are, my child. Have you been taking pretty-pills?"

Ashley smiled and shrugged, feeling her cheeks fill with color. "I was just daydreaming, I guess."

"A most excellent pastime!" Cassie complimented her. "Do you remember our good friend dear Henry David? Well, *he* said not to be afraid of daydreaming. He called it building dream-castles in the air. The only thing is, he said, we just need to put foundations under them. You do know how to build foundations, don't you?"

The girls hesitated, but Tiger piped up: "You mean with cement? Or bricks and stuff?"

"What a perceptive child you are, little prince!" Cassie told him. "Exactly! Block by block, brick by brick, we build up our foundations. For example, little Tigedore, if you thought you wanted to be an artist, what kind of blocks would you have to use?"

Tiger felt nervous. If he was really "enceptive" or "perceptive" or whatever it was Cassie had called him, why couldn't he think of the answer to her question?

"I really *do* want to become an artist," Brittany broke in exuberantly. Then she drew back a little, embarrassed that she had actually made the announcement.

"*Wunderbar!*" Cassie trilled. "A most wonderful daydream! And the dreaming and the wanting and wishing are very, very important. But if it's ever going to really come true, what must come next?"

"A foundation?" both Tiger and Brittany tried timidly.

"Absolutely, my dears! And what would be the foundation that would turn a dreamer-artist into a real one?"

"I guess you'd have to practice a lot," Brittany suggested. "You'd have to study and do a lot of drawing and painting and—"

"Oh my, yes!" said Cassie. "Those are the very bricks. If you want something very, very badly, then you simply must *do* something about it. How much, little sprite, do you really want that dream of yours to come true?"

"Well," Brittany began. "I sort of—"

"Oh my, little sweetheart," Cassie cut in. "I'm afraid 'sort of' just won't do."

"Well, I mean I *do*. If I just—somehow—knew that it could really happen."

"Things, you know, don't just happen," Cassie said. "Very few things in the whole world, pretty Brittany, simply *happen*. They happen, love, because we *make* them happen. It's like this old log we're sitting on. If we had waited to see if some tree might fall and block the road, do you think it would have happened in a million trillion years? No—we had to finally get our hands a little dusty and maybe get a sliver or two while we strained and tugged and dragged it inch by inch into its proper place. But it's here now. We *did* it."

"Do you know what I'd like to do?" Tiger asked.

"No," Cassie said, leaning toward him so that she looked at him face to face. "But I'm absolutely shivering with goose bumps to find out. Cross my heart."

"Well," Tiger began—and he swallowed and stalled, trying to think of an answer. A moment ago, it had seemed like a good question to ask, but now he wasn't sure what he had had in mind. Visions of firemen, mailmen, circus clowns, and cowboys did jerky somersaults in his head. Suddenly his mind latched on to a part of an idea, and before he had even thought it through, he found himself blurting out: "I want to be a robot."

Cassie's head bobbed a little, and she blinked her eyes. "A robot?"

"Yeah," he said shyly. "In outer space."

"Do you mean a—an astronaut?"

"No," he answered, swallowing again. "A robot."

"Well," Cassie said, as though now *she* were trying to stall for time. "What an interesting idea. I've never been very happy being a robot, myself."

"Were you a robot once?" he asked, wide-eyed.

"Well, yes and no," she answered. "Every time I find myself hooked into a routine, doing the same dull things over and over and over—without feeling, without caring—I'm afraid I've become a little too much like a robot."

"Well," Tiger began. "I guess I don't really want to be a robot. I just kind of said that."

"Of course, you can choose to be whatever you want," Cassie said. "But be very, very careful what you wish for—for it might come true." She looked at Ashley.

"And pray tell what shimmering castle is being constructed in *your* imagination, my lovely?"

Ashley squirmed a little. "I think I'd better wait. I'm just not sure."

"But you have dreams, don't you?"

"I haven't really thought about it," Ashley replied, trying to sort through her thoughts in search of a few shreds of a dream.

"Can you have more than one?" Brittany asked.

"Oh, my dear, you can have positively multitudes! But generally in different areas. Usually there's one main dream that we feel we must follow." She reached out and rubbed the back of her hand on Brittany's cheek. "Are you having second thoughts about your dream of being an artist?"

"No," Brittany answered quickly. And when she thought about it, she really meant it. "I was just wondering about other dreams — like how I want us to be — I mean, here in this house and stuff like that." *And about Rob,* she thought to herself, realizing that there must be a very important dream there, concerning her brother, that she would have to give some thought to.

Cassie was looking at her so intently that Brittany wondered if she was able to peek into her mind. Cassie smiled. "I'll write it down — along with all the other things I must do."

Brittany stood up straight, staring at Cassie. Was she really talking about finding a way to bring Rob there? "How — ?" Brittany heard herself saying weakly.

"Leave it up to me," Cassie said. "You see, *I* paint too. And if I can just find my watercolors when I go back into town, I'll smuggle them back and we'll start, you and I, seeing what we can do about your dream-castle."

Brittany blinked. It was all too fast. It wasn't Rob that Cassie was talking about at all, but becoming an artist. And yet — the thought made Brittany shiver. If Cassie was magic enough to help bring about the one dream, was there any reason why she might not be able to make the other one happen too? Especially if she, Brittany, helped put the blocks in place. And, even though this thought made her shiver again, she found herself smiling as well.

As they wandered back toward the clearing where the thick dark vines almost completely hid the cottage, Ashley too felt a little shiver run through her. "Oh, could we trim the vines just a little?" she asked as they stood at the edge of the clearing facing the abandoned dwelling. "Just enough that it won't look so —"

"Yes," Brittany urged, turning anxiously to Cassie. "So it's more like — like our home."

"But it *is* our home," Tiger said.

"Of course it is, sweet love," Cassie said. "And we'll make it just as beautiful as possible."

"And can we name it?" Ashley urged.

"Something like Green Acres or Green Gables —" Brittany began.

"How about Wildwood Manor —?" suggested Ashley.

"Those names all sound sort of — fancy," Tiger objected. "I mean it *is* kind of tumble-down."

"Then how about — Crumbledown?" Cassie twittered. And they all looked at each other.

"Doesn't that have just the right balance to it?" she went on. "Our little mansion may be a wee bit dilapidated but surely it's as worthy of a lovely name as any country estate one might find in England or Ireland —"

"Crumbledown," Ashley breathed, staring lingeringly at the wonderful cottage with its tipsy roof and crumbling honey-colored stone almost lost under the rich vines and towering hollyhocks.

"Yes, Crumbledown!" Brittany and Tiger cried almost at once.

"Then Crumbledown it is!" Cassie whispered warmly.

*C H A P T E R*

*8*

Even before the afternoon was over, Ashley had already decided that this was the longest day of her life. Not *boring* long—like the dull Saturdays at the Oglethorpes when it was too cold to play outside and the TV was off limits until their chores were done—but wonderfully long, the kind you wished could keep going on forever.

Lying on her back in the grassy shade under a tree, Ashley tried to remember the whole day. How impossible it was to think that it was only last night that they had opened their eyes and first discovered Cassie sitting on Tiger's bed! Now that moment seemed centuries away.

What a morning it had been—from waking up and seeing the first warm rays of sunshine, to eating fresh berries by the brook, to cleaning Crumbledown, to hearing stories of famous operas and nibbling the last of some crackers and cheese Cassie had found in the bottom of one of her sacks, to learning about famous artists like Michelangelo and Leonardo da Vinci while exploring a more dense and rugged woods west of the small enchanted one that bordered on the cottage.

The afternoon had been filled with games—guessing what the clouds resembled as they slowly transformed their billowing white outlines into strange new shapes, making wreaths of tiny flowers for their heads, watching for fish in the stream where the water slid like silk over the smooth shiny stones.

Ashley rolled over on her stomach, giving her long gown a tug or two so it wouldn't bunch up uncomfortably under her. She was wearing the silky rose-colored one with the feathers now, for she and Brittany had traded earlier before their hike into the forest. She reached up to her hair and caught one of the deep pink flowers that had begun feeling loose whenever she turned her head. It was looking a little wilted now, and she felt a funny feeling in her stomach because she wanted everything to stay as beautiful as it had been all day. Was it all going to wilt? Would someone come and find them there and spoil everything? She shook her head quickly, wanting the thoughts to go away.

She jumped suddenly, startled by the sound of footsteps running toward her.

It was Brittany, the skirt of her blue-lavender gown clutched up in her hands so she wouldn't trip, the wreath on her head slipping down over one eye. "I wondered where you'd gone to," she sighed, out of breath. "You should see the cottage now. If Tiger doesn't stop bringing in more flowers, it'll turn into a greenhouse!"

"I thought it was almost perfect how it was," Ashley said, still feeling a tinge of melancholy.

"Oh, it's perfect. Almost, anyway." Brittany's smile

faded. "I just wish—I wish my brother could be here with us." Ashley swallowed, feeling a sudden little shiver. *No, she thought to herself. No one else. It's too perfect as it is—and someone else might spoil everything.*

They looked up to see Cassie and Tiger, hand in hand, coming toward them. "Guess what?" Tiger called. "Cassie said that, in just a little while, we get to go meet Cow!"

Ashley cocked her head, looking up at Cassie. "I don't get it," she said. "When you told us about—about Cow— you made it sound as if a cow with black spots is something really great, something—"

"Oh, it is, it is—believe me!" Cassie gushed. "You just haven't been reading your Emily Dickinson, my love. Emily Dickinson, you see, was a poet—and oh, what a poet she was!—and she told us that the song of a bird might be a common thing or something absolutely divine—depending on how our ears are made."

Without even thinking, Tiger felt one of his hands sneak up and feel his ear. "How do you think mine are made?" he asked.

"Oh, gloriously! No question about that!" Cassie exclaimed. She looked at Ashley, then Brittany, then Ashley again. "And yours, as well—am I right?"

Brittany felt that she too wanted to reach up and touch her ears. "How can you know?" she asked.

"Why, it's easy!" Cassie said. "Just take this simple little test: when you step on the grass, does it squeak and whisper little messages to you? When a cool spring breeze sets a spider's web trembling and quivering, do you hear the shivering of a harp: Do you see pirate's ships and plumed serpents in the clouds? Does the smell of damp pine needles make you feel the shady coolness of springtime? Does the touch of dry, crackling leaves make you taste October?"

Ashley felt uncomfortable. "I don't see what smelling and tasting have to do with how your ears are made," she mumbled.

"Oh, yes, my dear!" Cassie responded. "It all has to do with how we're put together — eyes, ears, nose, mouth, fingers! But even more," she whispered, "it has to do with how you're made inside — with how the real you that lives way down inside you can be sensitive — and absolutely alert — to every smell and sound and — "

"Are you talking about the morning that's in us?" Brittany asked.

"That's it!" Cassie said. "Be one of those on whom *nothing* is lost,' Henry James once said."

"Wow!" Tiger breathed. "You sure do know lots of people!"

"Especially for being allergic to them!" Brittany couldn't help adding.

"Oh, it's only the ordinary people I'm avoiding right now, remember," Cassie said. "Henry James and Emily Dickinson and dear Henry David Thoreau — they were absolutely *extra*ordinary, like you — with extraordinary feelings and thoughts. They were the ones on whom nothing was lost. Oh, my yes—there wasn't a taste or smell or a sound that could slip by them. But let me tell you a little secret," she whispered. "Even the ordinary people are extraordinary. They just don't know it."

"Maybe we could tell them," Tiger suggested.

"What a beautiful idea!" Cassie exclaimed. "Help me remember that, little Tigedore. We'll have to write that down soon so we don't forget it: TELL ALL THE OR-DINARY PEOPLE THAT THEY'RE NOT ORDINARY AT ALL; THEY JUST NEED TO BE VERY VERY AWAKE!"

"Except maybe sometimes they could sleep—just a little bit," Tiger tried to help.

"Well, I'm not sure," Cassie said. "If they plan on dozing or nodding off at all, then they'll certainly have to make up for it by being *extra* alert when they're awake. Right?"

"Right!" Brittany answered, smiling.

Cassie sighed, looking off into the late afternoon sunlight. "The minute the sun squeezes itself between that hill and eternity, I must disappear."

The children blinked at her in unbelief.

"To Chesterton," she added quickly, with a slight smile. "And if I don't leave early enough, it will take me the whole night to get there and back—and we have a long list of things I must find and bring back with me. It'll be like a scavenger hunt, you see."

"Oh, can we go?" Brittany asked.

"Please!" Ashley begged.

"Oh, no, no, no, my dears!" Cassie crooned. "It's enough of a chore just for me, sneaking along the hedges and hiding behind bushes. Oh, goodness, no! Besides, if I didn't return, *you* would need to be here to be in charge of Crumbledown!" She looked at Ashley, then at Brittany, and smiled. "But trust me, sweet loves—I *will* come back!"

"Are you going to walk all that long way?" Ashley asked her.

"A goodly part of it," Cassie answered. "Oh, but I do hope I can find a ride like last night. I must be very, very careful, though, you see, and I need to go in some kind of disguise. They just may be looking for me in Chesterton. Even though I never actually lived there, I did hibernate there with a friend for a while, near that little church I told you about, and maybe they'll be on the lookout. Last night," she whispered, "I caught a ride with a pick-up truck, pretending I had just got off the bus coming from Littlefield on its way to Fairmont. I told them I was visiting my niece in Chesterton."

"That sounds like us!" Brittany exclaimed, remembering how the lady named Mrs. Finlayson had dropped them off at the make-believe birthday party.

"Your job, while I'm gone," Cassie was saying, "is to block out the windows in the cottage, fix yourselves some supper, and then get right to bed so we can get up early.

But first, since I'll be gone, you'll need to keep our rendezvous with *La Vaca*."

"With who?" Brittany asked.

"*La Vaca*. That's Spanish for *cow*. Now it's true that Cow and I didn't say much to each other yesterday afternoon, but I'm no fool when it comes to accents, and if that wasn't a first-rate, authentic Spanish 'moo' that Cow gave me yesterday, then I'm a pickled parsnip. Just remember," she went on, "to say, *'Buenos tardes,'* when you approach her—and don't forget—"

"But how will we milk her?"

"Come!" Cassie said, taking the pail from Brittany and shooing the girls toward the cottage like Old Mother Goose with two of her flock. "I'll show you—and then I must be gone!"

They hurried through the long grass and wildflowers to the cottage where Tiger played on the doorstep with tiny figures made from leaves, grass, and twigs. Within a few minutes Cassie had disguised herself in the coat with the fur collar Tiger had worn the night before and a strange brown hat with a wilted feather. She quickly folded three paper bags and stuffed them in her pockets, then motioned to the children to follow her through the fields.

The sun was already partially hidden behind the distant trees now, but there was still enough daylight that Cassie cautioned them to crouch low as they hurried across a field, slithered under a wooden fence, then crossed a dusty lane and crawled beneath the barbed wire of a second fence. And there, on the edge of a vast, grassy pasture, Cassie paused suddenly, spreading out her arms to hold them back. She seemed to be listening for something. Ashley looked at Brittany, then at Cassie. Tiger took hold of Cassie's coat.

"Just stay low," she said. "We're almost there."

They crept along the fence where wild bushes grew in splotches and kept them hidden from the adjacent field. Coming to a corner, they crawled under a wooden fence and suddenly found themselves in a green pasture where four or five cows grazed lazily.

"There she is!" Cassie whispered. "That's Cow!" And she pointed to a beautiful spotted cow who raised her head and stared at them as she went on chewing a mouthful of grass.

"*Buenos tardes,*" Cassie called in a whisper. "We've come for some *leche*. That's *milk*," she explained to Tiger. "Now you, little prince, you and Brittany stand guard. If you see anything or anyone, crouch low and hoot like an owl. Ashley, bring the pail and come with me. They'll warn you if anyone comes."

She and Ashley tiptoed toward the cow who continued to stare at them dumbly. "*Que guapa,*" Cassie crooned, caressing the cow's nose and resting her cheek against its velvety neck. "This is Ashley, Cow. She'll be gentle — so just be calm and try not to put your foot in the milk pail." Then she knelt down and placed the white pail in front of her, under the cow's bulging bag with its four pink teats.

Ashley shuddered. "Yuck," she murmured. "Do I have to touch those?"

Cassie smiled. "Yes, princess. But think of it as magic. With just a trick of your hands—and a few 'abracadabras'—your empty pail will be filled with fresh warm milk!"

Cassie pulled gently at one of the cow's salmon-colored teats but nothing happened. She tried once again; still nothing happened. She turned to Ashley and forced a little smile. "Maybe we both need to say the magic words: *abracadabra gelida manina!*"

Feeling very foolish, Ashley tried to repeat the words after her: *"abracadabra gelida manina . . ."*

And again they tried, repeating the words slowly and softly in unison, while Cassie tried each of the four teats. But it was only when she tried the first one again that a sudden little stream of milk, spurting out at an angle, caught them by surprise.

"There! You see?" Cassie beamed. "Now, I must be off!" She gave Ashley a quick little kiss on the cheek, waved hastily to Tiger and Brittany who crouched by the fence, still watching intently in opposite directions, and then she sneaked across the field, burrowed under a fence, and was gone.

Ashley swallowed and reached out a timid hand to touch the soft pinkish-orange udder, half-expecting that

Cow might jump or bellow out a terrified Spanish moo. But there was no sound. Neither was there any milk. Ashley closed her eyes, gritting her teeth again, giving a gentle tug. Nothing happened. Oh, why did this have to be *her* job? Why not Brittany's or Tiger's? Tiger would probably love it. But then they'd know that she had been afraid. Maybe she could just tell them that Cow didn't have any milk tonight—except that Cassie knew. But she could always tell Cassie that Cow had stepped in the pail and spilled the milk . . .

Not feeling good about telling a lie, she closed her eyes again and reached out, determining to get milk this time. Still nothing happened.

"Oh, please, Cow!" she murmured through her teeth. *"Buenas tardes,* or whatever!" Then she remembered the magic words: *"abracadabra gelida manina . . . abracadabra gelida manina . . . "*

A little squirt made a hollow sound in the bottom of the pail.

"Hooray, Cow!" she almost cried out. And she began working vigorously with both hands, first one teat, then the other, the alternating streams of milk making two separate sounds as they squirted against the inside of the pail.

"Oh, Cow—I love you!" Ashley sang out. And then she wondered how you would say that in Spanish.

"I'm actually milking a cow!" she announced to herself proudly, letting her forehead rest against Cow's soft furry side as she continued the rhythm of the milking. Suddenly Cow moved and Ashley gasped, first with surprise and then with the fear that the pail was going to be tipped over, but she managed to catch it just in time.

"Oh, dear," she said, wondering how to start again after Cow had finally stopped a few feet further on. But just as she picked up the pail and started toward her, Ashley became aware of a strange sound—something monotonous and annoying, almost like the sound of an owl.

An owl! She perked up and stared behind her. "Hoo! Hoo!" Tiger was hooting anxiously, his face scrunched up in terror as he pointed off through the bushes toward the wooden fence.

Ashley gasped. Someone was coming!

Ashley snatched up the partly filled pail of milk and fled to the corner of the field where Brittany and Tiger huddled in the bushes against the fence.

"Look!" Brittany whispered. Peeking through the leaves, they could see, on the other side of the fence, a tall lanky farmer in overalls striding across the field toward them.

"Crouch down!" Ashley urged. They shrank back into the bushes as he came nearer and then passed momentarily out of sight. Then, hearing him fumbling with the gate just a few yards away, they inched back into the dark shadows between the bushes just as the gate creaked open and shut and he walked past them in the direction of Cow.

"Hee-ah! Get a move on!" he growled, waving his arm and herding the cattle off toward the other end of the pasture where there was still another gate and what looked like the roof of a barn and maybe even a farmhouse beyond.

"He's probably going to milk them," Ashley said softly, trembling as she wondered if the farmer might have some way of knowing that Cow had already been partly milked. Hugging the pail against her, she whispered to Brittany and Tiger that now might be a good time for them to try to escape. Without wasting a second, they scooted under the fence and hurried off across the grassy meadow.

"Wait!" Ashley panted. "Do you think we're going right?"

Brittany shrugged uneasily, looking around her. The darkness was coming on quickly, and all she could tell was that they were standing in the middle of a huge field bounded by fences.

"Do we go that way, I wonder," Ashley said, pointing to where the fence seemed nearest, "or is it more *that* way?" She looked off in the direction of the hills where the sky still held what Cassie would have probably called just a "whisper" of pink.

"Are we lost?" Tiger asked, feeling scared.

Ashley held the milk pail firmly against her chest as though it might keep her heart from beating so fiercely. The feathers of the rose-colored gown felt damp against her chest where some of the milk had splashed.

"We should have looked better," Brittany began to whimper. "I wasn't really paying attention when we came."

"Ssh," Ashley said, motioning them to duck down as a faraway grumbling noise grew louder and a pick-up truck came rattling down a dusty road on the other side of the far fence. When it had gone and only a cloud of dust hung in the dimness, Ashley whispered loudly: "That's the way! We crossed that little lane, remember?"

They ducked under the fence then crossed the narrow lane to the fenced-in-field with new green plants growing in tidy rows. But just as they crawled under the second fence, Tiger squealed, startling Ashley so much that she almost spilled what little milk was left.

"Look!" he cried, pointing toward the shallow ditch surrounding the field. "Look what I found!"

There, almost hidden in the tall grass between the ditch bank and the fence, was a makeshift nest with four large white eggs.

"Get them!" Ashley said. "That could be our supper!"

Brittany hesitated: "But what if—what if they're just about to turn into baby chickens?"

"The hen probably wouldn't have left the nest if she had been sitting on them long enough to be ready to hatch," Ashley said, hoping her reasoning was right. "Besides," she went on, "I'll bet the eggs were there just for us. Cassie said she felt that Cow was *our* cow, and maybe she made arrangements with some chicken—*our* chicken—to lay—"

"Really?" Tiger asked. "Do we have a chicken too?"

"Maybe," Ashley said, almost beginning to believe it herself. Suddenly she pictured the four of them posing on the doorstep of Crumbledown for a kind of family portrait, surrounded not only by vines and flowers, but also by a lively mass of chickens and ducks and goats and geese, all of them theirs.

Tiger and Brittany each picked up two eggs and then the three of them marched off across the field. Ashley led, keeping her eye on a group of trees in the distance that she hoped would be their own little woods.

When they crawled through the last wire fence, it was a relief to find that the trees not only looked quite familiar, but they could also hear the gurgling of the stream and even make out the faint outline of the cottage against the greenery beyond.

"We're home!" Tiger cried. And Brittany felt her velvet gown rubbing against Ashley on one side and Tiger on the other giving her a warm and satisfied feeling inside. Crumbledown really did feel like home — and Tiger and Ashley felt like her real brother and sister. Only Rob was needed to make it absolutely complete. And — of course — Cassie. A tiny shiver rippled down her spine, and she found herself saying a little silent prayer that Cassie would not get caught by the police or hit by a car or break her leg in some ditch.

They entered through the back screen door and almost without a word set to work blocking out the windows. Then, making sure the front and back doors were also closed and pushed into place, they lighted a fire. As the flames grew, the room itself seemed to take on a color almost like melted butter. Feeling so pleased they could hardly speak, the three of them glanced at each other, big smiles overtaking their faces.

Their supper was a rare treat. Even though the milk tasted lukewarm and strangely cow-like at first and the eggs kept sticking in the bottom of the little pan they had placed near the coals, they found that scrambling the eggs and warming the milk made the most memorable supper they had ever had.

As the fire died down, they grew drowsy and would have almost fallen asleep there in front of the warm, glowing coals if Ashley hadn't suddenly reminded them that they all really did have "beds." In their housecleaning earlier in the day, they had agreed that the small room at the end of the front room would be Cassie's since she had found it first, and they had all helped move the newly dusted cot in there for her. For *their* bedroom, Ashley and Brittany had settled on the room that might once have been a kitchen and made soft mattresses for themselves out of grass and leaves. The little room next door had been declared Tiger's room, and he too had worked on a tidy mound of long grass covered with a burlap bag where he intended to spend his nights.

Yet it looked different somehow by night. They only had to glance at each other as they stood on the threshold of the back room to know that they were all thinking the same thing, and, in a flash, they had brought all the makings of their various mattresses into a corner of the front

room and arranged it all into one large but neatly orga-
nized bed.

"How else could we have shared the quilt?" Tiger
asked as he snuggled between the two girls and curled
up, pulling the oatmeal-color sweater down to cover his
toes. He rested his cheek against Brittany's shoulder and
felt happy that he not only had one sister but two. Ashley
really was a good big sister. Sometimes she scolded him
and sometimes, at the Ogelthorpes', she begged him not
to play with them. But he remembered all the times she
had taken care of him — all those long afternoons in the
big brick apartment house in Rupert City that smelled
like sour milk and wet diapers. For a moment he thought
of his mother's face — pretty, but too pale, even with all
the make-up. He never understood how she used to
squeeze him and ask him if he thought she was a good
mama, and then she would be screaming and throwing
things, and then kissing him and crying. He could still
remember the smell of her hair and her perfume. But he
could remember the heavy smell of cigarette smoke, too,
and the sweet but stale smell of whatever it was that she
drank that made her act crazy.

His grass bed smelled fresh and moist and felt cool
where it touched his ear and his neck. Whatever kind of
wood was burning in the fireplace smelled good too —
almost spicy. Cassie would be happy that he wasn't missing that smell. He didn't want to miss anything. He
breathed deeply to make the grassy smell come back into

his head and help him to dream of trees and meadows and hills sprinkled with soft woolly lambs . . .

Something soft was touching his cheek. He stirred, trying to make his way back from the grassy meadows of his dreams to the room where someone was tucking the quilt around his neck. Suddenly he sat up, but something gently pushed him back.

"It's the middle of the night, little prince," a voice whispered soothingly.

And he rolled back on his side to breathe again the fresh grass and to smile to himself that this time it wasn't a witch at all that kissed his cheek, but the most wonderful fairy godmother in the whole world — or in any other world.

## 10

"Look what Cassie brought!" Tiger announced excitedly the next morning. And Ashley and Brittany sat up to see Tiger, still in the big woolly sweater, nestling a snowy white kitten against his chest.

"I just couldn't resist," Cassie chirped from where she stood near the fireplace, arranging a bouquet of fresh yellow flowers. "But, oh, my dears, how many times I almost let him go! He jumped out of the basket trillions of times on the way back and I had to search him out of the bushes in the dark?"

"Lucky he's white!" Tiger said.

"How did you come back from Chesterton?" Ashley wanted to know. "Did you get a ride?"

Cassie's eyes widened and a mischievous smile began to creep across her lips. "Oh, my sweet lovelies — I simply floated all the way back! No, not floated — flew!"

The three of them stared at her, waiting for the explanation. She was wearing a faded green blouse covered with so many tiny scallops that it looked as if it might once have been part of an artichoke costume. Her skirt was actually a beige corduroy bedspread trimmed with brown fringe and tied at her waist with a man's green-

and beige-striped tie. Her hair, wound loosely on top of her head, was held there with a home-made crown of leafy vines.

"You want to know how I flew?" she asked, leaning forward so that her face was inches away from Tiger. "What do you think, Nicholas?" she whispered to the white kitten in his arms. "Do you suppose we really ought to tell?"

"Tell us!" Tiger urged, finding himself whispering as well.

"Well," Cassie began, "of course you *do* believe in flying broomsticks . . . "

Ashley glanced at Brittany and they both immediately rolled their eyes.

"—and magic carpets!" And she threw out one arm with a flourish, her hand pointing toward the open doorway. "Go see for yourselves, unbelievers! Believe that you'll see broomstick, magic carpet, and spectacular flying machine all rolled into one, and what you see will dazzle your eyes. There! Behold Lancelot!"

Cassie swirled her bedspread skirt across the threshold and stepped out into the grass so they could all peek out. There, under the nearest tree, was a strange conglomeration that looked part machine, part animal, and part Arabian Nights.

"What *is* it?" Brittany asked.

"That, my dears, is Lancelot," Cassie announced proudly.

As they all moved slowly toward it, Ashley and Brittany and Tiger studied the bizarre combination of items that made up this so-called "Lancelot": its frame was basically that of a bicycle, although it had been sprayed gold and decorated with sparkling red and gold Christmas tinsel. The seat was a pony saddle, also sprayed gold. Hanging from the back wheel and almost completely covering it was a deep red velvet tapestry with a foreign peasant scene in gold, blue, and purple, the whole thing trimmed with gold fringe. Mounted on the gold fender above the front wheel was a stuffed parrot with its wings spread and slightly battered, and above that, where the handlebars should have been, was a set of velvety moose antlers.

"We've weathered many a storm together, haven't we, Lancelot?" Cassie asked, stroking the strange contraption.

"You mean—you mean that's what you ride on?" Ashley asked in unbelief. "Where's it been?"

"Well, we've actually only known each other for a matter of hours," Cassie said. "We really just met last night, you see—and yet, believe me, after our long and adventurous flight in the dark, Lancelot and I have become quite marvelous friends."

"Was there a storm last night?" Brittany asked.

"Storm?" asked Cassie.

"You said that you and Lancelot had braved many storms together and—"

"Oh, my sweet dear, those were storms of a different color!"

"What color were they?" Tiger asked.

"What I mean, little Tigedore, is that Lancelot and I had some of the most wild adventures last night, flying along the highway with only the moon to guide us. At least twice we were attacked by road bandits," she said, holding up one arm to display a scraped and bruised elbow.

"Is that really true?" asked Tiger.

"Why, most certainly! Of course, they disguise themselves as holes in the road or strange little bumps that run you off into the bushes. With no lights on Lancelot, Nicholas and I had to fear for our very lives, didn't we, dear thing?" And the cat meowed as if in agreement.

"Luckily the moon was out," she went on, "because when the moon is full the way it was last night, the little road gremlins seem to disappear, and sometimes Lancelot and I could sail along in the most heavenly way, without fear of phantoms or headlights."

"Headlights?" asked Tiger.

"Oh, yes, my dear—dragons of the most dreadful sort!" She looked at Ashley and Brittany. "Whenever a car appeared on the road, I simply couldn't let them see me, you understand. So whenever those two angry burning eyes appeared down the highway, I had no choice but to simply slow down and pull Lancelot off the road and hide us in the shadows. Very tricky, you see—but I don't think anyone spotted us at all—except once—oh dear me! — when I simply couldn't get off the road in time and a carload of boys nearly frightened me out of my wits. And Nicholas, too," she added. "That was one of the times when poor Nicholas was so terrified he leaped out of the bag and ran off into the trees and it took me more than twenty minutes to find him."

"I can't believe you really made it back!" Ashley said, worried about Cassie's bruised arm. "Don't you think it might be better to walk than to have to — " and her voice trailed off as she looked over in the direction of the old contraption called Lancelot.

"At times I was beginning to wonder, my dear," Cassie confided, smoothing her hand across the rich velvet covering draping its back. "But when we soared through the night, it was absolutely heavenly."

"Wow!" Tiger said, hardly able to breathe. "Where did you ever get it?"

"It was a miracle, my child, believe me. After I got into the church — and I had to slip through the window this time — I found so many things for our little cottage that I had filled up four huge bags before I scarcely had time to blink my eyes. And that was before I went back to the Montagues' where I used to stay — to look for my watercolors!"

"Did you get them?" Brittany asked eagerly.

"I certainly did! And my nice big pad of watercolor paper too. They were right where I had left them in the closet of the guest room. And I found a pair of my shoes there too. Although when I looked at them this morning, I discovered they don't match. Rummaging around in the dark, I must have taken one of mine and one of Bessie Montague's. Oh dear—"

"Didn't anyone see you?"

"Bessie doesn't hear well and was in bed, I'm sure—and her daughter Hilda must have been away somewhere since her car was gone. But the door inside the garage had been left unlocked, and I just slipped in like a quiet little mouse and found all my things."

"Aren't you going to be in trouble for taking all those things from the church?" Brittany asked.

"Heavens, no," Cassie replied. "Most of them were things of mine, like I said—things that I had given away because I thought I had no more use for them. And the other things—well, maybe we'll have to think of something we can take back as a trade before they get around to having the next rummage sale."

"I've been thinking about the milk we took last night," Brittany said.

"And, guess what, Cassie! We found some eggs, too!" Tiger put in.

Brittany went on: "About the milk—I think maybe we should think of a way to pay back the farmer."

"A wonderful idea!" Cassie agreed. "But it will have to be terribly secret!"

"You mean like leaving brownies or cookies or something on his doorstep?" asked Brittany.

"Or maybe flowers—" suggested Ashley.

"Or what if you got him a new suit or something from the church?" Tiger wondered.

"Oh, more secret than that, I'm afraid. You see, with all his cows, he probably won't notice that one cow has a little less milk than usual—but if he suddenly starts getting elaborate gifts on his doorstep, he's going to become very suspicious—and, the first thing you know, we'll be discovered. But, you're absolutely right, we must pay him—someway—in return for the milk. Let's write that down, love—and very soon we'll put on our thinking caps and—" Suddenly she stopped and looked at Ashley. "You were able to get the milk then—with no trouble?"

"Oh, yes," Ashley said, proudly. "At least a little bit. But I'm afraid we drank it all—every drop!"

"And it was *so* good," Tiger said. "Especially when we warmed it up!"

"Well, tonight," Cassie said, "you must get us much more—so that we'll have enough to pour on our berries in the morning—and enough that I can make some fresh yogurt. You see, I must confess that I sneaked just a smidgen of yogurt from Bessie's fridge—and I think it'll be just enough of a starter for us to make a nice batch of our own."

"Yogurt sounds yucky," Tiger said.

"Oh, but little prince—you must never say that until you've tried it. And tried it again and again. The very best things you don't always like right at first. And usually when we say we hate something, it just means we don't know enough about it yet—that we aren't quite familiar enough with it yet. Some things take a little getting used to—but when you grow to like them, I can guarantee you that you'll like them oodles longer than something that seems good right off but then begins to get a little too sweet and intense and—"

"Like Halloween candy, right?" Tiger asked. "I think I've still got some in my drawer at Oglethorpes' that I couldn't ever finish."

"Exactly, little prince. How wise you are! And you will love Cassie's yogurt. We'll try it with berries and we'll try it with—"

"But what if I can't get enough milk?" Ashley broke in, cutting her off. "I think maybe *you* should milk Cow tonight so that we'll—"

"Oh, my dear," Cassie exclaimed, interrupting Ashley. "I would so much prefer that *you* be our little milkmaid. After all, you did it so well and—" She paused and looked at Ashley almost as if she were embarrassed. "Would you believe, Ashley love, that I've never milked a cow in my entire life?"

"But you were the one that *taught* Ashley last night—" Brittany started.

"Oh, my—I'm afraid I faked that, dear one," Cassie replied. "These hands of Anastasia the Great would never have been allowed to touch a beast of the barnyard, I'm quite certain of that ! Oh, no, my dears, when Cassandra du Maurier tried to milk Cow last night, I assure you it was for the very first time."

"But you did it!" Brittany said. "You know how!"

"I certainly never could have done it if I hadn't tried, could I?" Her voice grew very soft: "Let me share a secret with you: even though I was a famous actress, known and praised throughout the world, for nearly fifty-five years, I told myself that, because of the particular way my fingers seemed to be built, I could never snap my fingers the way other people do. Oh, I rubbed them together furiously, but could never make a single pop — never a sound of any sort, except a feeble rustling of my thumb against my finger. And then, one day, a young man heard me say how it was absolutely impossible for me to snap my fingers, and he said, 'But ma'am, you're doing it the wrong way. Don't just rub the tip of your finger against your thumb — rub the inside of your knuckle!' And I tried it — and the whole world turned around, It really did. Can you imagine what excitement ran through me when I discovered, at the age of almost sixty, mind you, that I really *could* snap my fingers — with a pop as sharp and loud as anyone else's? Believe me, that revelation awakened a good deal of the morning in me! I wanted to run and jump and do handsprings and somersaults — for what else, I suddenly wondered, might I be capable of performing?"

She turned back to Lancelot and ran her hand over the velvety smooth, flat moose antlers. "That's why I didn't hesitate to try to mount dear Lancelot here. When I found how many bags I had finally accumulated, I knew I could never carry them all the way back here. So I found Lancelot, tied my bags to his antlers, and away we flew!"

"And hadn't you ever ridden a bicycle before either?" asked Ashley.

"Just remember, sweet lovelies, there isn't much that Cassandra du Maurier has not yet tried—not since I learned to snap my fingers, at any rate."

"Have you even ridden elephants?" asked Tiger.

"Elephants," pondered Cassie. "Let me see . . . well, if I haven't, I certainly must, mustn't I?"

"How about camels?" Tiger wanted to know.

"Listen, sweet Tigedore. If you'll come with me back to the cottage, first, I'll show you what I've brought for our breakfast! Aren't you absolutely famished? Secondly, I'll lead you all to another secret place I've never taken you. And third—I'll tell you, once and for all, since you're so very full of questions, the whole story—the exciting, adventurous, incredible story—of Mademoiselle Cassandra du Maurier!"

And the four of them flew back to the cottage.

They sat on the hillside in a ring beneath a gigantic oak tree that spread above them like a fresh green parasol. Below them stretched the whole panorama of the valley — from the bluish-green strip of trees that would be the outskirts of Chesterton to the fields where Crumbledown almost blended into the woods and finally to the main road spread out ribbon-like across the landscape.

Cassie peeled an orange, sprinkled cinnamon on a plump juicy slice, and then let it drop into Tiger's open mouth. Anxious to hear Cassie's story about herself, Brittany watched her carefully, trying to imagine how she might have looked fifty years earlier riding Lancelot down the street in one of her elegant gowns.

"I would love to begin at the beginning," she announced, "if only I knew what the beginning really was. I'm afraid I can't honestly remember Czar Nicholas II, who may have been my father, and I'm not even sure I can remember St. Petersburg and Moscow and the palace — although, if I try to think very hard, I can almost imagine how it must have been. But I do remember my dear Uncle Anton with his elegant handlebar moustache and shiny gold pocket watch that hung on a long chain and was kept in the pocket of his gray-striped vest. He used to take me to the park and let me ride the carousel or listen to the band concert. And sometimes he bought me ice cream that was the color of the full moon and felt exactly like satin on the tip of my tongue."

She hesitated a moment, smiling even though her eyes were closed, her body almost swaying as if keeping time to some invisible orchestra playing a waltz. "He was the one who took me to Bombay and Cairo and Tangier," she went on. "And one time that I'll never forget — although I'm not sure if we were off the shores of Normandy or taking a steamer down one of the fjords in Norway — but I can remember so plainly sitting on the deck of the ship, perched atop a gigantic coil of rope while the sea-breeze blew my hair. I wore a marvelous little black velvet beret on my head and held in my arms the most wonderful striped cat . . . "

Tiger closed his eyes, trying hard to picture every detail. Suddenly he sat up straight, wondering what had happened to their own cat, Nicholas. Then he remembered seeing him sleeping in the sun that filtered in through the back window.

"Isn't a beret a hat like artists wear?" Brittany asked.

"Exactly, my love! And, of course, we must get you one, my dear. I brought the watercolors and paper — but how silly of me not to have found you a beret. Well, we'll just have to put that on our list, won't we?"

Again Cassie's eyes drifted shut and she continued

to smile. "How I loved that day — sitting on that coil of rope with my cat while the wind blew through my hair. Uncle Anton took me there many times. And then — when I was about sixteen — I went to Budapest. That's in Hungary — and did you know it's really two cities, divided by a river? Buda is one one side, sprinkled over the hills, and Pest is on the other, across the bridge. But where was I? Oh, yes, we were fleeing from the secret police in Eastern Europe, my brother and I — twins, can you believe it? Cassandra and Sebastian. Sebastian and I had been warned that we had been recognized one day on the streets of Budapest as the descendants of Czar Nicholas II, and suddenly the streets seemed to be filled with guards and soldiers everywhere. There was absolutely nothing we could do, but try to escape — in disguise. And we made it to the seacoast of the Black Sea — but then something quite terrible happened!"

"What was it?" Tiger interrupted before she had time to go on.

"There was the most dreadful storm at sea — billowing waves and such a ferocious wind tossing the boat to and fro that it finally overturned, spilling us all into the angry sea. How long we thrashed about in those incredible waves I'll never know. But we clung to an oar or the remains of a splintered raft until, finally, we were washed ashore, one of the sailors and I. But my brother — my poor sweet Sebastian — was lost at sea along with the rest of the crew, and though we searched the horizon for any sign of them, we could find nothing—absolutely nothing. Oh, my little one, can you imagine what it's like to lose your brother?"

Brittany almost wanted to interrupt and say, *Yes, yes, I do know,* but instead, she just swallowed and went on listening.

"And do you know where we were? Sicily. We had been washed ashore on the island of Sicily, off the coast of Italy, where the houses are all whitewashed and cling to the edge of the cliffs among the olive trees and orange groves. Well, of course, I was just thankful as a ripe plum that I was alive—but, oh, my dears, at the same time, I was simply terrified out of my wits to find myself so suddenly alone in such a strange and lonely country. Remember, I was just a young girl—not too much older than our Ashley here—and frightened beyond belief. But I got an idea. Some of Sebastian's clothes had been washed up on the beach with the wreckage—yes, a wooden chest with some of Sebastian's things had drifted ashore, and I immediately changed into them to keep dry—the way you did with my clothes night before last. And can you guess what happened next? I not only felt more bold dressed as a young man—but people on the island immediately fell for the disguise and took me completely for a boy. And do you know what happened? I was hired as a young messenger for the Duke. Can you believe it? It was fantastic! Suddenly I was there living in the palace, serving the duke, and delivering messages to a most wonderful young woman—Olivia, she was called—and the Duke, of course, loved her so very very much. But—the most strange thing happened. Can you imagine what it was?"

None of the children spoke, but they continued to stare instead at their storyteller.

"Well, I think Olivia loved the Duke—a little at least. But as I continued to deliver more and more messages of love from him to her, a most unusual thing happened: Olivia, little by little, began to be drawn to me—dressed, as I was, of course, like a dashing young man! Well—can you imagine what a mess it was all becoming? The Duke, now, was madly in love with Olivia, and Olivia, poor thing, thought she had fallen in love with me, and I, my dears had discovered that I was falling in love with the Duke! But that's not all. Oh, no! Sebastian, you see, turned out not to be dead after all! No, not at all: he had been washed ashore on another part of the island and soon showed up at the palace looking so much like me that both the Duke and Olivia didn't know whether they were talking to me or to Sebastian or seeing ghosts or—"

Suddenly she stopped, sitting up very straight. "Listen," she whispered, her eyes suddenly darting about. "Speaking of ghosts—"

Ashley, too, straightened up, straining to hear what Cassie seemed to be hearing.

A man's voice, from far away, was calling, "There they are—over there!"

"Oh, no!" Brittany murmured, feeling her body wanting to shrink and hearing Tiger make a little whimpering noise beside her.

"They've found us," Ashley whispered, realizing that the most beautiful moments of her entire life were about to be snatched away from her.

## *12*

None of them moved an inch. They hardly breathed, in fact, as they watched two figures appear on the top of the hill above them. Brittany felt the tears well up in her eyes until the figures—a tall man and then a shorter one carrying a rope—were only a blur.

"Look!" Cassie whispered. And Ashley continued to look, still not believing her eyes. The taller man pointed off in the direction of Chesterton, and then the two of them hurried in a jagged diagonal down the hillside, each step taking them further and further away from the oak tree.

"Maybe they're after the horses," Ashley breathed, noticing that, far away, against some low bushes, a brown horse and its colt nibbled at the grass.

"You mean they weren't after *us?*" Tiger asked.

"I guess not, my love," Cassie whispered, her relieved sigh echoed by each of the other three. "Well," she said, sprinkling cinnamon over the last slices of orange and holding them out to the children, "we'll continue our stories later. I'm afraid my heart's a little too fluttery right now for me to think quite straight. It feels as though I've got a hummingbird—or a woodpecker—in my chest."

Watching to make sure the two figures with the horses had totally disappeared from view, they then made their way down the hill and across two grassy meadows to Crumbledown.

For Brittany, however, the frightening experience on the hillside did not go away easily. Even as she giggled with Ashley and tried on the clothes Cassie had brought, she still couldn't shake completely the nervousness that gnawed at her like a hungry and persistent little mouse.

But she liked the grown-up dress Cassie had found for her — a soft, silky blue-green with a silvery sheen — even though it reached all the way down to her ankles, and she especially like the elegant feather boa Cassie showed her how to loop around her neck.

Ashley's dress was a slinky dusty maroon crepe with 1940's shoulder pads and a pale rose drape that hung from the shoulder. Tiger, from the odds and ends Cassie brought him, chose a pair of knickers the color of cinnamon which, even hitched up high under his sweater, drooped almost down to his toes.

By the time Cassie had shown them every item stuffed into the four bags she had brought back on Lancelot, Brittany began to feel better, and the thoughts of that morning's narrow escape evaporated from her mind. She was especially excited about the set of watercolors and pad of paper that Cassie pulled from her bag between the mismatched salt-and-pepper shakers and the fat ball of string. But for Ashley, the most exciting items were a thick notebook and pencil that Cassie had brought for her and an amber-colored chenille bedspread and a slightly yellowed lace tablecloth which Cassie said they could cut up for curtains. Next to Nicholas the kitten, Tiger liked best a somewhat battered clown doll that Cassie promised could be made into a puppet.

"It will be absolutely *wunderbar!*" she told him. "That means *wonderful* in German."

"Voonderbar! Voonderbar!" Tiger cried out, dancing around in his baggy new corduroy pants. "You're better than Santa Claus, Cassie!" Suddenly he stopped. "Didn't you bring anything for you?"

"Why, of course!" she replied. "Don't you like my new outfit?" And she whirled around, modeling the beige bedspread skirt and the artichoke-costume top. "And not only that! When I went back to Bessie Montague's to get my watercolors, guess what I found among my things in the closet?"

She pulled out a long thin package with colorful designs on it from between the pages of the watercolor pad. "Do you know what this is?" she asked, opening the package. "It's incense! Three delicious aromas — jasmine, rose, and sandalwood." She lingered over the words as she pronounced them until Ashley felt they were all on the verge of being transported by magic carpet into some faraway exotic land.

Cassie slipped one long slender green stick from the

package, and carried it to the rough mantel of the fireplace where the matches were.

"Where will it be?" she asked, striking the match then hesitating before lighting the incense. "Bombay? Baghdad? Bangladesh?" And Brittany too felt as if the room itself were about to rise up and go whirling through the air beyond Munchkin Land to some foreign spot at the ends of the earth.

Cassie lighted the incense, then blew out the flame so that only a narrow thread of smoke curled upward. "Today," she said, closing her eyes and breathing in its spicy scent, "today it will be Kashmir ... "

Somewhat reluctantly, the children too, one by one, closed their eyes as Cassie's voice went on. "There— can you hear the tinkling of the brass bangles the girls wear on their arms? Can you feel the soft swish of the silken saris as they pass you in the market place? Can you smell the curry and saffron? Can you hear the wheels of the carts pulled by oxen through the tiny streets?"

Ashley felt a prickly shiver on the back of her neck. *If this is Kashmir, let me stay here a little longer,* she repeated to herself. Then, suddenly, she was aware of a voice—Brittany's—worriedly asking, "Cassie—are we— are we taking drugs?"

Cassie's voice was like the tinkling of the glass bracelets they had imagined: "Heavens, no, my dear one. An ounce of imagination is far more precious than a ton of drugs! It's just that smells have the power to create a

mood for you—or bring back a distant time or place."
They all had their eyes open now and Cassie went on:
"One day, my sweets, you'll walk into a room and smell
something—like fresh bread baking in the oven or hot
spiced juices simmering on the stove—and it will send
you somersaulting into 1922. Or—for you—maybe February the thirteenth—five, six, maybe seven or eight
years ago!"

"What happened on February the thir—" Brittany
started to ask.

"Oh, who knows, child? I only made it up. I simply
mean that, maybe for you, the smell of hot rhubarb pie
might bring back an afternoon long past—and for a minute, maybe just a second or two, you will be able to hold
onto it, before it slips back through your fingers and loses
itself once again in the long ago and far away."

Brittany and Ashley looked at each other, and each
tried to think of a smell that would bring back the past.
"Here," Cassie said suddenly, quickly snuffing out the
still-smoking incense with two fingers. "Let Kashmir go.
Let's try someplace different. How about Bavaria?"

"Bavaria?" questioned Brittany. "Where's Bavaria?"

"Did I go there one time?" Tiger asked. "How can I
make it come back if I didn't ever be there?"

"Oh, my dears—there are so many games we must
play! One game would be to bring back all the times and
places we've known so long ago—but another game could
transport us to places we've never been yet! We'll call

them travel games. Cairo, Copenhagen, Kathmandu —
we'll visit them all! Emily Dickinson said you could create a whole prairie in your mind — as long as you had
one clover and one bee — and of course, plenty of imagination. In fact, she said, if you couldn't find a bee, the
imagination alone would do it. And it's true! We can sail
to Burma, scale the Himalayas, or cross the Khyber
Pass!"

"How about Disneyland?" asked Tiger.

"Oh, most definitely!" said Cassie, enthusiastically.
"And Java and Gibraltar. And Singapore and Siam — except
that Siam is no more."

"What happened to it?" Tiger asked. "Where did it
go?"

"Oh, the land is still there," Cassie explained, "but
it's called Thailand now. Like Persia — which we no longer
call Persia but Iran — or Ceylon, which we now call Sri
Lanka. But let me tell you a deep secret. *We* can travel
back in time — and visit them all when they were still
Siam, Persia, and Ceylon! I always wanted to sail to Byzantium while it was still Byzantium and not Constanti-
nople or Istanbul as it became later — so we absolutely
*must* plan a trip there too."

"How do you know so much, Cassie?" Brittany
gasped.

"Oh, my dear — there's so much I *wish* I knew! But
time is so short — and the world is so very full! It's like
one gigantic Christmas stocking! But do help me remem-

ber, at least, to find time to get back to studying my
Norwegian and Arabic. I found my books at Bessie
Montague's, you see," she said, pointing to a fat blue
book and a smaller red and orange one stacked among
the treasures unloaded from the shopping bags. "That's
one of my goals—to read Norwegian plays and Arabic
poetry in the original languages!"

"But I don't get it," Tiger said. "I thought the 'goal'
was some place you run to when you play hide and seek
or something like that."

"Oh, it *is*, little Tigedore, it is! Goals are the places
we're trying to get to. And I'm afraid I've got so many
I'm almost dizzy. But here's what we'll do: we'll all pick
someplace we want to go—something we want to get
done—or something we want to become. And we'll scribble it down. That's important!"

"Do we have to scribble?" asked Tiger.

"Well—no," Cassie smiled. "But we must write it
down. And then—we must *do* it! Remember Thoreau's
castles? They're goals—it's as simple as that!"

"But what's *my* castle supposed to be?" Tiger asked.
"I forgot."

"Oh, Tigedore, dream castles aren't *supposed* to be
anything. They're whatever you want them to be. But
it's important that you really care about them," Cassie
said. "My castle," she went on, "or at least one of them,
is to not let a day go by without watching the sun rise
and smelling each new blossom and noticing every lady-

bug or dragonfly. And Brittany's, remember, was to become an *artiste!* And we're going to work on that this very morning, aren't we, love?"

Brittany nodded, a little feeling of excitement beginning to grow inside her.

"And Ashleykins—have you been able to conjure up a goal yet?"

Feeling herself squirming inside, but trying to remain calm, Ashley shook her head quietly.

"No hurry, love," Cassie said cheerfully. "But let me whisper one little goal for you for the rest of the morning. Take this book," she went on, placing a thick notebook and pencil in Ashley's hands, "and go wherever you wish. But please write down all the wonderful things you see and think of—and how you feel about them. Pretend those exquisite blue eyes of yours are seeing everything for the very first time—and then write down what you discover."

Ashley hesitated. What Cassie wanted her to do sounded very difficult, yet the very challenge sent a strange shiver through her body.

"And what will my goal be?" asked Tiger.

"Let's start by seeing what magicians we can be, you and I," Cassie said. "Don't you think we can take this limp and flimsy little clown doll and—"

"And turn him into a real live boy?" Tiger belted out, enthusiastically.

"Well—" Cassie stammered, "—almost! Do you suppose you could settle for a real live marionette?"

"Okay," Tiger agreed, bright-eyed.

"Take your notebook, then," Cassie said to Ashley. "And you, Brittany, take these watercolors and the pad of paper down by the stream somewhere where you have plenty of water and try *all* the colors. Find how they look by themselves and how they look when you let them run together or when you mix them. Don't be bashful, love — experiment! Then, as soon as Tiger and I finish here, I'll come down and see what you've discovered. Off with you, then!"

And off they went.

While the morning sun filtered down through the leaves and vines overhead, Brittany experimented with the watercolors, excited how the colors would seep into the thick paper and then merge slightly with the surrounding tints, forming new shades of color she had never dreamed existed.

Tiger and Cassie, meanwhile tied strings on the head, hands, and feet of the Pierrot doll, turning him into a wonderful marionette almost as if they had breathed some kind of life into him. And Ashley sitting by herself in the shade of the trees, pondered how she might describe in her new notebook the way three fat little toadstools looked like three Chinamen gossiping under the brims of their coolie hats.

Cassie ran back and forth among the children, chirping compliments like some joyful bird. Once when Brittany looked up to see her coming through the trees, her arms were loaded with something dark and moist and green.

"Look, my love—watercress!" she exclaimed. "It's all along the riverbank—food for woodland nymphs and water sprites. We'll sprinkle salt on it and you'll love it!"

Brittany looked at Cassie, and a warm feeling came

over her. Had they really only known her for two days? No—not even quite two days yet. It was hard to believe; it seemed as if they had known her forever.

"What thoughts are being born behind those beautiful, beautiful eyes?" Cassie asked. "Blue pools so deep and large I could almost swim in them."

Brittany wanted to speak—but there seemed to be no words that could express how she felt inside. Surely there was no one in the world quite like Cassie. Was there anything she couldn't do?

"Cassie," she suddenly heard herself saying as she sat upright. "Cassie—do you think—do you think you could help me find my brother?"

"Do you mean little Tigedore?" Cassie asked, looking puzzled.

"No—not Tiger. He's not my—well, he really is my brother, I guess—sort of—although he's really Ashley's little brother more than mine. But, you see, I do have a real brother—a grown-up brother, named Rob—who's almost fifteen, I think. And I haven't seen him for a long time—except for a few minutes last winter when he came by my school on his bike one day to give me a Christmas present. It was recess and I just happened to be out playing on the monkey bars."

"Where can you find him?" asked Cassie.

"That's the problem. I'm not really sure—and I'm afraid he might have moved and then I won't ever be able to find him. He told me the name of the people where he *was* staying, though—and it's a name like Elmer or Helmer or something like that. Maybe Hellam or Hillam or—"

"Oh, dear me, sweet Brittany—if only you knew the name for sure—"

"Well, I tried not to forget it. I really think it is Helmer or Helman or Hillam or—" Suddenly she broke into a sob. "I feel so awful that I don't remember—because now he'll never know where I am and—"

Cassie held her close. "Oh, we mustn't cry, my sweet little one. I'm sure we can do *something!* Do you have any idea what town he's in?"

"Oh, yes," Brittany said, sniffling, but trying not to cry. "I'm pretty sure he's still in Chesterton—*somewhere.*"

"Well, then, we'll find him. Tonight we'll have our baths and I'll rest up from all my little tumbles in the bushes—and those attacks, you know, from all those frisky little road gremlins. But *tomorrow* night—tomorrow night, sweet Brittany, you'll go with me—and we'll take Lancelot and a bushel of good luck—and we won't come back until we've found your brother."

Brittany couldn't believe her ears. "Do you mean it?"

"My dear—! Does Cassandra du Maurier say *anything* she doesn't mean?"

And Brittany threw herself against Cassie's chest and cried the happiest tears of her life.

The rest of that day spun by in a whirl of events:

gathering watercress from the grassy banks of the ditch; cutting out and sewing by hand enough amber chenille and yellowed-lace curtains for every window in the cottage; learning a Portuguese folk song in three parts and how to say "Thank you" and "Good morning" in five different languages; bathing by moonlight in the cool stream; making the fresh yogurt in a covered pan by the fire; and finally hearing Cassie tell the stories of *Les Misérables* and *The Hunchback of Notre Dame* and listening drowsily but happily as she sang them a lullaby in Balinese.

The next morning found them up before daybreak and coming home from an adventurous morning walk not more than an hour later, their arms loaded with crisp rhubarb and more of the deep-green watercress. After a delicious breakfast of yogurt and berries, they finished the puppet stage, complete with curtains and scenery, and started work on two new puppets made from scraps around the cottage and Cassie's ball of string.

Before long Brittany was at work with her watercolors again and Ashley was back in the woods recording her impressions of the morning in her notebook; Tiger and Cassie, meanwhile, scampered off to gather tiny sticks and plants to make a miniature forest for the puppet stage. And as the morning passed, they played games in the woods and then carried home bouquets of wildflowers.

On their way they spotted more of the fish in the

stream that Tiger had seen earlier, and soon they had set about devising their own fishing pole: the same twine used for the puppets was wound around a broken chair leg and fastened, at one end, to a bent safety pin disguised by a wiggly worm. For a long time it looked as if all their hard work was going to be for nothing, but finally they happened upon a spot in the stream where the fish began nibbling at the worms almost as quickly as they could put them on. If more got away than they were finally able to pull into shore, the children still came scrambling back to the cottage with three medium-sized fish and two small ones, which Cassie helped them clean and then wrap carefully in a cool cloth to store in the shade until suppertime.

Next, Cassie took them back to the little clearing in the woods where the berries grew, and they spent the rest of the afternoon acting out scenes from plays. They sat spellbound while Cassie herself did parts of *The Glass Menagerie* and the sleep-walking scene from *Macbeth*. Then she sat back and made up character after character which Ashley, Brittany, and Tiger took turns bringing to life, imagining as they went, how each might look and what kinds of things they would do and say.

"Oh, please — let's not stop!" Tiger begged, after Brittany had just finished a turn pretending to be a princess transformed by a sorcerer's spell into a wild silvery bird.

But Cassie said they'd have to continue playing it again another day. "It's getting late, you see," she went on, "and little Brittany and I have to get ready for our secret mission."

Once again Ashley felt the little tug of disappointment, even though Cassie had carefully explained the plan the night before when she had tucked them in their big grass-cushioned bed and sung them lullabies. "It'll be much faster—and much safer—if just the two of us go," she had said. And Cassie was right, Ashley knew that. Still, she couldn't help feeling just a little left out.

"And you, Ashley dear," Cassie said, her eyes looking once again almost as if she were peeking into Ashley's mind. "I have a special job for you. First you and Tiger can check for eggs and get our milk again—for you're the one with the magic touch, you know, But then, while Tiger works on his puppets and prepares a special show for all of us tomorrow afternoon, I want you, dear Ashley, to concoct for us the most marvelous, the most fantastical and beautiful play you can come up with. Three acts, five acts, whatever you wish—and we'll start rehearsal on it tomorrow. Write for me any part you wish—but make it superb—and very challenging! And, you know, my love, it really wouldn't hurt to include a part for a young man— for, if all goes well," she said, winking at Brittany, "we'll be bringing home a guest!"

Wide-eyed, Tiger looked up at Cassie, then he remembered what she had told them at bedtime the night before. Two different feelings bumped against each other inside him: he wanted Brittany to be able to find her brother, but he wasn't sure, at the same time, that he wanted anyone else suddenly barging in on their happy little family here in the woods.

"Well," Cassie suddenly announced, "soon the sun will be napping, and Brittany and I must get Lancelot ready for the trip so that we can leave just as soon as it gets dark."

They hurried back along the little path to the cottage that was now beginning to become familiar. Crumble-down, still smelling faintly of incense, was just as they had left it. Nicholas, the cat, was curled in a fuzzy white ball against the deep purple corduroy bed the girls had fixed for him in an old box. He blinked his eyes once as they came in, then went on dozing in the gold-spangled rays that fell through the window across the hearth.

Cassie gave each of them a job—Brittany was to work out a disguise for herself, changing her silky gown for Tiger's sweater and knickers and tucking her hair up into a floppy cap that Cassie brought home two nights before; Tiger, dressed now in a large T-shirt that hung clear to the floor and had faded red letters across that had once read COLONIAL WILLIAMSBURG, was to accompany Ashley across the fields to see if Cow had milk for them and if the chicken, whatever its name was, had left behind any more eggs. Cassie, meanwhile, volunteered to get the fresh fish from where they'd hidden them from Nicholas and prepare the hearth for a fire so that, at the very moment it began to get dark, she could darken the windows and start frying the fish for their supper.

Daylight was finally disappearing into night when Ashley and Tiger crawled under the last fence and scurried home across the fields with half a pail of milk and six fresh eggs (which Tiger carried by stretching out his enormous T-shirt in front of him to make a soft cradle for them). It had become dark enough by the time they neared Crumbledown that they smelled the smoke from the chimney before they saw it, and, with it, the inviting aroma of fish sizzling to a golden brown on the fire.

"Oh, bless your hearts, my little muffins!" Cassie exclaimed joyfully when she saw not only milk but eggs as well. Soon they were all chattering as they nibbled away at the delicate bones of the delicious fried fish. And while they savored the tangy-sweet flavor of hot rhubarb which Cassie had prepared for dessert, she put the eggs on to boil, explaining that they would put them away with the milk somewhere cool (and safely away from Nicholas!) until morning. This way they would be able to have a cooked breakfast without running the risk of someone spotting the chimney smoke by daylight.

"It's a good thing we found six eggs instead of just four like last time," Tiger said proudly, "just in case you really *can* find Rob and bring him back." But again he felt a strange little feeling stir inside him. He looked around the room, glowing golden-warm by the hearth's fire. Would one more person somehow spoil it all? He swallowed, thinking—and half praying—that maybe they wouldn't be able to find Brittany's big brother after all.

"Be a sweet little prince," he heard Cassie saying, "and help your sister with the dishes. You'll need to get more water from the stream, Ashley. And remember," she added, giving Tiger a soft little pinch on the cheek as she slipped her arm into the big wool coat with the fur collar that Tiger had worn that first night in the cottage, "put the good china in the china cupboard with the crystal, and sort the silverware nicely on the buffet."

"The what—?" he was about to say when he caught the reflection from the fire sparkling in Cassie's bright eyes. It was another one of her jokes, he decided. He liked that. A family needed more jokes. There hadn't been many at the Oglethorpes' house—and even less at the big brick apartment house in Rupert City where his mother had smashed bottles and mirrors and then sobbed behind locked doors.

He and Ashley watched as Cassie and Brittany wheeled Lancelot from its camouflaged hiding place in the trees. Tucking the last strands of her silvery hair up under her brown hat with the wilted feather, Cassie kissed them each on both cheeks and gave them last-minute instructions. "And don't forget to keep all the windows covered," she added, balancing Brittany on the gold-painted crossbar with its Chrismas-tinsel decorations. Even in the dusky light, they could see Lancelot teetering dangerously as Cassie got on and then pedaled wobblingly away. "Farewell, my loves—pray for us!" she called back through the darkness, and the strange vehicle and its two riders jiggled and zigzagged down the lane until they finally dissolved into the blue night.

Ashley breathed deeply, realizing that she must have been holding her breath almost since the two passengers had begun to mount the fearless Lancelot. Tiger, too, echoed her relief with a deep sigh of his own that turned into what seemed like an endless yawn.

"Aren't you tired?" he asked finally, reaching out to hold Ashley's hand. "What day was it we made the puppet theater? Was that yesterday?"

Ashley had to think for a moment. "Was it yesterday? Wait—no, it was this morning—this very day!—before we went fishing, remember?"

"It seems like another day, doesn't it? How long have we been here at Crumbledown, anyway?"

Ashley tried her best to count the days but lost track and gave up. "I don't even know anymore," she announced. "But it seems almost like forever." And she felt happy when she said the words.

"I hope it *can* be forever," Tiger said, giving her hand a little squeeze as they walked back to the cottage and slipped inside.

"Do you feel too sleepy to work on your puppet show?" Ashley asked him as they knelt down before the smoldering fire.

"Well—not really," he told her, realizing that, when

he actually thought of playing with the puppets, he really wasn't all *that* tired. He felt Nicholas nuzzling against his knee, and he pulled the purring kitten into his lap.

"I'm going to work on my play," Ashley announced. "But first I just want to write down in my journal some things about today. Cassie says we should keep a journal of all the things we do and feel." She paused, looking at Tiger and Nicholas, lighted by the fire. "I can help *you* do one," she added, " – if you want."

But suddenly she raised a finger to her lips, her eyes, wide with fright, darting quickly toward the window. "Be quiet," she whispered. "Listen!"

Tiger stopped breathing. Not even daring to turn his head, he let his eyes slowly move toward the front door and the windows with their coverings carefully placed to block the light. "Who is it?" he finally whispered, hearing, even as he said it, a faraway rumbling noise, then a voice. "Is it Cassie and Brittany? Did they come back?"

Ashley didn't answer. Her eyes drifted slowly back and forth as she strained to recognize the distant sounds. Suddenly a muffled noise – like the thud of a car door slamming shut – jarred them both.

"What'll we do?" Tiger whimpered, clutching Nicholas tightly up under his chin as he crouched, trembling.

Ashley hesitated, then whispered breathlessly, "Come on! Let's slip out the back way or they'll catch us!"

Snatching Tiger by the hand, she leaped up and the

two of them—Tiger still squeezing Nicholas against his chest—tiptoed quickly through the little room at the rear and then slipped noiselessly out the back door. The night air made them shiver, and they huddled together in the deep shadows behind the cottage before moving further.

"—down this way somewhere," a voice beyond the trees seemed to be saying.

"Oh no! Are they looking for us?" Tiger managed to whisper weakly, his hand trembling in Ashley's.

"Wish we had a light of some kind," a voice, faraway, called out.

"Turn the car lights back on a minute," another shouted back.

Tiger felt Ashley grip his hand and then pull him forward. As quietly as they could, they slipped between the bushes and over some fallen branches. Suddenly he felt her pulling him downward and, for a moment, they crouched together soundlessly in the tall grass at the edge of the grove of trees. Beyond the silhouettes of the trees they could see the figures of two men moving in and out of the dusty shafts of light cast down the lane from the headlights of a car.

"—wanna try and move this log?" one voice called.

Mumble. Snapping of twigs. Then something about "Leave it. This has got to be the wrong road anyway. Looks like it's turning into some lousy cow path." Silence. Snapping of twigs again. Coughing.

Suddenly: "D'ya smell what I smell? Somebody's got a bonfire around here." Muffled reply.

Then: "Hey. I think I know where we are. Didn't there used to be an old house somewhere back in here?"

Mumble. Then something about "torn down or falling to pieces."

"Smell that smoke? That's a campfire!"

"Nah, it's probably coming from a wood stove in one of those farm houses. I think I smelled it way down the road back there."

Tiger closed his eyes. *Pray for us,* Cassie had said. But who was going to pray for *them?* He squeezed Nicholas tighter up under his chin — but it must have been too tight, because the kitten suddenly meowed.

"D'ya hear that?"

"Hear what?"

"Sounded like a cat or somethin'."

Mumble.

Tiger let go of Ashley's hand and tremblingly soothed Nicholas's furry head and neck.

"You're too jumpy, Sagers. First you see something with two heads riding down the road on a moose —"

"C'mon, you saw that as well as I did — only you thought it looked like two people flying by on a parrot." Laugh. Silence. Then: "You got anything left in that bottle?"

" — all you need, you lousy bugger." Mumble. Sound of moving around.

Ashley's fingers gripped Tiger's shoulder, forcing him to stay low.

"Where d'ya think yer goin'?" they heard one of the men say.

Mumble — and the grumbling sounds growing louder, nearer.

Suddenly: "What in the —?"

And Tiger and Ashley, drawn together so that their separate trembling merged into one terrified shiver, tried in vain to melt into the ground as the snapping of twigs became louder and louder and they felt the large figure looming suddenly above them.

The air felt cool against her cheeks as Brittany clung to the moose-antler handlebars, the stuffed parrot perched proudly in front of her and Cassie huffing rhythmically behind her.

"Do you think I should try to pump *you* for a while?" she asked timidly.

"Oh, fiddlesticks!" Cassie breathed, in between huffs and puffs. "What do you think I am? A helpless old woman?"

"No! I just meant that — well — I *am* eleven years old now — and one time I pumped Tiger," Brittany said. "It was just around the block — but I didn't even feel very tired at all." She was all ready to say how they had only tipped over a couple of times, but then decided maybe she wouldn't mention that.

"Hang on tight, sweet love," Cassie sang out, still puffing away, as a set of headlights appeared out of the blackness far ahead of them. "We'll just take another little detour and enjoy the scenery once more —"

Just then Lancelot wobbled and swerved, then bumped through the bushes and weeds until they came to a jolting halt and toppled over on the side of what

126

seemed to be a grassy embankment. Brittany thought she could still hear Cassie breathing heavily as they fell back on the long soft grass, but she leaned over straining to peer at her face in the dark to make sure she was all right. Just then the car with the headlights zoomed by on the road above them, and, for a second, Brittany could see Cassie, her hair half tumbled out of the felt hat and her eyes closed, but her face relaxed in what seemed to be a happy smile.

"Are you all right?" Brittany ventured.

"Am I all right?" she crooned. "Don't you know, sweet cupcake, that Cassie du Maurier will always be all right if she can just rest her head on the fresh clover for a minute and wink back at all those precious little stars up there." She gave a long sigh and then went on softly: "We huff and puff through life—like you and I were doing—sticking carefully to the main road until one day something forces us off and we discover quite another path—less traveled is the way Robert Frost, the poet puts it—a path where we can take our time and smell the fresh night air and listen to the water chortling to itself in the stream down there somewhere—"

"I was afraid we were going to go right down the side and *into* the stream!"

"Mmmmmm," Cassie hummed. "Wouldn't *that* have been refreshing? What delicious ideas you have, *ma petite.*"

"What does '*ma petite*' mean?"

"That means *my little one* in French. My precious little one," Cassie said, putting her arm around Brittany and pulling her close. "Ah me," she sighed. "My own Uncle Anton used to cuddle me like this when I was about your size. He's the one, you remember, who first took me to Rangoon and Singapore — long *long* before I became a famous actress, you see. And I would sit on the deck, holding my cat, with the wind blowing through my hair—"

"You told us," Brittany reminded her.

"Ah, yes," she sighed. Then still holding Brittany close, she began singing, very softly, one of the little lullabies they had heard her sing before:

> *Toora loora loora*
> *Toora loora li*
> *Toora loora loora*
> *That's an Irish lullaby . . .*

Another car whizzed by overhead.

"Ready to tackle it again?" Cassie asked, rising up.

"Maybe we ought to just walk for a while."

"Splennnndid idea!" Cassie exclaimed. And, one on each side, they pushed Lancelot back up onto the road and walked along the edge of the darkened highway, smelling the wild honeysuckle and listening to the crickets.

It seemed like hours of walking then riding, walking then riding again, before Brittany finally spotted the lights of the town. "Is that it?" she cried. "Isn't that Chester-ton?"

"Either that—or Camelot," Cassie whispered. "Or maybe it's Shangri-la . . . " Lancelot slowed down to a stop and Cassie slipped off the seat, helping Brittany down as well.

"*Regardez,*" she said. "We'll be nearing the moat in just a teeny bit—"

"The moat?"

"Oh, yes. Almost every walled city has one." Brittany tried to picture either a wall or a moat in Chesterton, when Cassie spoke again, this time softer. "*Regardez, ma petite!* There! Can you see it?" She pointed off into the darkness. "We need to turn off here before anyone sees us. Besides, down there," and she pointed off to the right once again, "that's were we'll find the only place we can cross the moat safely."

Still straining her eyes to penetrate the dark clumps of trees where lights twinkled beyond, Brittany clung to Lancelot as Cassie guided him to the right until they found themselves turning down a small dark lane. Brittany could hear the river running now and realized they were fol-lowing it along the outskirts of town, purposely avoiding people and traffic. And from the moment Cassie started telling the story of the opera *Carmen,* Brittany noticed that nothing interrupted them; instead of approaching headlights, they passed only the soft lights of farmhouses along the way.

Cassie had hardly completed her tragic tale of the gypsy Carmen when she pointed off to the left to a little white bridge where another country road crossed not only the road they were on but the river as well. "That's it," she said. "That's the only drawbridge that will take us safely inside the walls."

By now Brittany was smiling to herself — although she did still feel a little sad because of what happened to poor Carmen and Don José. But it cheered her up to think that, as long as she was with Cassie, even turning down a dirt road and crossing a little bridge seemed like a major adventure. Despite how tired her legs were beginning to feel, she was glad they had come this way instead of staying on the highway and crossing the main bridge of town. They had not only avoided being exposed by the glaring headlights of the town's traffic, but, in the dusky shadows of the outskirts, it was easier to believe they really were on the verge of invading some long-lost kingdom.

As they turned left and crossed the bridge, passing a dark barricade of tall poplars on each side, she could almost imagine that they were truly slipping beyond the sturdy walls of a medieval fortress and that, when they would finally discover where Rob was — and they simply *had* to find him! — he would be dressed in tall boots and a feathered hat like Robin Hood or Romeo and would cry out with joy to them from some tower cell or secret dungeon. Suddenly, Brittany's eyes focused on the actual lighted houses they were passing, and she wondered how close they really were to the section of town where Rob had been living.

Within the next few minutes, they had to scoot Lancelot three times into the shadows of a hedge or bush while a car or pickup passed them, but when the fourth car started down the street toward them and then turned, they spotted in the sudden flash of its headlights a darkened telephone booth.

"Have you thought of the name yet?" Cassie asked anxiously. And Brittany closed her eyes tightly, as she had done so many times on their journey this night, in a last effort to bring back the name that Rob had told her when he had visited her on the playground that wintry day. "I just don't know for sure—but I still think it might be Hillam or Hillman or something like that."

They wheeled Lancelot across the street and into the shadows of a drive-in hamburger stand that looked as if it had been closed down for years, then fled toward a phone booth partly lighted by a street lamp further down the road.

"How will we ever read the numbers in the dark?" Brittany asked anxiously. Then a worse thought struck her: "Do we even have any quarters?"

"Hold the door open," Cassie directed, while she peered into the dusky booth. The telephone itself, Brittany suddenly noticed, seemed to have a tattered paper dangling from it by a piece of tape.

"What's this?" Cassie asked, trying to uncurl the edge of the paper with her hand while tilting it so that the light from the streetlight fell on it. "Could it by any chance be a coded message from Rob the captive?" she asked. "Or do you suppose it might be some kind of a trap?"

Brittany's heart leaped. A message from Rob? How *could* it be? Then her eyes made out the dismal sign with its faded, homemade lettering: OUT OF ORDER.

"But there's a phone book," she suddenly cried. "Or at least part of one." Together she and Cassie reached for the dark rectangle, its shabby pages protruding, dangling by a chain. At the same instant, they both squeezed back inside the booth as first one car and then another passed by. When it was safe again, they opened the door to take advantage of the streetlight while they fingered the few water-warped pages in the telephone book.

Now Brittany's heart sank. Almost every page had been ripped out. "Vandals and barbarians," she heard Cassie murmur half to herself.

"Couldn't we at least search the scraps?" Brittany asked sadly. "Or maybe look for another phone booth?"

Cassie hesitated a moment then tugged at the little triangles of paper remaining in the book. "Absolutely, little hummingbird—we'll search the scraps! After all, love, we only need to find one name—if it's the *right* name!"

Clutching the fragments, they scurried from the booth, ducked once into shadows to let a car pass, then huddled under the street light further down the block. Cassie tilted her head back, holding two or three of the little corners of paper at arm's length. Brittany, taking a handful, held them close, squinting to read the fine print.

"Miller, Milner—M's!" she said, putting that one on the bottom and looking at the next. "Naylor, Neal, Neeley—"

"E's," Cassie was mumbling. "Look—! No, that's the G's. Wait—here it is—H's! Here we are—" she began excitedly, but then Brittany heard her voice suddenly drop. "Oh, shenanigans!" she muttered. "The only H's readable—and there are only half a dozen I'm afraid—are not the H I's. All that's left of this page starts with"—she paused—"with Hegstrom or something like that. And this one," she said, turning to the next scrap with a sigh, "starts with Ingersoll!"

Just as Brittany felt a wave of disappointment welling up inside her, she glanced down at the scraps of paper Cassie was shuffling in her hand. Even in the dim light of the street lamp, a name near the top of the H page seemed to jump out at her: there, below the names of Heiner, Heinz, and Hellewell, loomed the name *Helmes*.

"Cassie, look! What about Helmes?"

"Well, it—" Cassie suddenly stopped stuttering and looked at her. "You tell *me*, little dumpling. Is that it? Is that the magic name?"

Brittany squinted her eyes and looked at it again. "It *could* be. Hillam ... Helmes ... ," she mumbled to herself. "Yes, it could be! Can you read the telephone number?"

"Better than that," Cassie said. "Helmes, Leslie R., lives at—let me see—at 1034 Willow Lane. Willow Lane . . . ," she murmured quietly. "Unless my memory or my eyes are playing little games on me, love, we *passed* a Willow Lane not more than five or ten minutes ago. If the good fairies are really with us, child, we are right in the very neighborhood of Willow Lane. Quick, get Lancelot and off we'll fly!"

They scampered into the shadows as a car came by and then they waited there while three teenage boys strode noisily down the street. As soon as they had gone, they found Lancelot and pedaled off anxiously into the night.

"Of course," said Brittany, "it really *might* not be the right place—" But she scrunched her eyes up tight and said a little prayer to herself while Cassie huffed and hummed a little song behind her.

When they found Willow Lane, they only had to pedal two or three minutes down the street—long enough to find they were going the wrong direction!—then five or six minutes *up* the street, a black dog chasing and yapping behind them most of the way, before they came to 1034. The porch light was off, but there was light coming from the two front windows as well as a very dim one from a small window near the ground.

"The dungeon, probably," Brittany whispered jokingly, pointing to it.

"Unquestionably!" Cassie agreed. "Sneak over to it and peek in, while I tiptoe around this way and see what's going on elsewhere in the castle."

Brittany moved as noiselessly as possible toward the low, rectangular opening with its faint blue-gray light. The sound of muffled voices came from within. Inches away from the window, she peered down into the basement room.

It was mainly dark, but a small portable TV cast an eerie glow over a rumpled couch with a plaid cover. A figure in corduroys lay sprawled across it with one stockinged foot propped among the clutter on a coffee table.

Brittany's heart gave a leap. It *was* Rob!

## CHAPTER
## *15*

Before she had even checked to see if there were others in the room, Brittany found herself tapping frantically on the basement window. Rob glanced up from where he lay on the couch at the same time that someone else in the room—a figure lying on the floor in front of the TV—stirred and sat up.

"What's that?" Brittany heard a voice say just as she ducked back away from the window's stream of light.

"I don't know," she thought she heard Rob say. "Someone's playing around outside."

Bending forward just enough to get a partial view yet not enough to fall into the path of light, she thought she saw the figure on the floor twist back around and settle down again on the rug in front of the TV. Just then something touched her from behind.

She whirled, too scared to scream.

It was Cassie!

"Sssh!" Cassie cautioned, drawing her close against her, as if to calm her. Not sure whether it was her own heart or Cassie's that pounded in her ears, Brittany nevertheless jumped when she heard a door open just a few feet away from them. They quickly leaned back into the shadows of the house.

"What's going on?"

Trembling, Brittany turned her neck just enough to see the figure standing just outside the front door on the darkened porch.

"Who's there?" it said.

"Rob!" Brittany cried out when she realized who it was. "It's me—Brittany!" And she leaped out of Cassie's grasp and ran to him.

"Britt!" he said, startled, as she threw her arms around his waist and pressed her cheek against his chest. Cassie stepped from the shadows long enough to whisper a harsh "Shh!" just as a deep voice from somewhere inside called out, "What's the matter out there?" Brittany's finger went to her lips to echo Cassie's "Shh!" as Cassie pulled her down from the porch into the shadows.

Rob hesitated a minute, as though puzzled, then stepped back inside the front door. "Just someone playing around," they heard him tell someone inside. "Kids, I think."

Cassie snickered quietly, and Brittany gave her hand a little squeeze. Then they heard the front door close. When a minute or two passed and nothing happened, Brittany turned to Cassie anxiously. But before she could speak, they heard a faint click as the front door opened again softly and saw Rob slipping soundlessly off the porch.

"Britt!" he whispered. "What are you doing? Where have you been? I read in the papers how you'd—"

"The papers?" Cassie whispered.

"The police have even been here and—"

"Oh, Rob!" Brittany interrupted. "Rob, we're safe—safer than we've ever been—and so happy, Robbie—so happy you won't believe it. Rob, you've got to come with us—you've just got to!"

She looked up to see Rob's eyes staring at Cassie. "Rob, this is Cassie—the most wonderful—"

"Cassandra du Maurier," Cassie whispered elegantly, reaching out her hand as though she almost expected it be kissed. Rob hesitated awkwardly, his mouth hanging open, but Brittany quickly reached up and pressed Cassie's hand warmly against her cheek.

"Oh, Robbie, you've *got* to come back to Crumbledown with us! It's so beautiful—we're in a cottage by the woods—and Cassie has the most wonderful ideas and—"

"Come," Cassie whispered in a voice so low and throaty that it sounded almost as though she were casting a spell that pulled him like a magnet.

"I don't know," Rob said, swallowing and looking nervously back toward the porch. "I'd—I'd have to put some shoes on—and maybe get a couple of things." He looked back at the porch again. "Is it—far? Do we have to walk or—"

"We have Lancelot!" Brittany chirped.

"We fly!" Cassie echoed in her hoarse whisper. "But Lancelot might not be used to you," she added even more softly. "You might want to bring a bicycle . . . "

Rob swallowed again. "I have a bike. I mean, there is one that—"

"Hurry, then," Cassie urged. "And you can either pack a few things in a little bag or take pot luck with what we've got in the cottage."

Bizarre pictures flashed through Brittany's mind: Rob trying on the dusty-blue feather boa or trying to fit into Cassie's artichoke costume.

"Better bring a shirt," Brittany put in hastily, "and maybe a sweater and—"

"And perhaps a little blanket or quilt might come in handy," added Cassie.

"But hurry, Rob, please!" Brittany urged. "I'm scared that those people in there are going to—"

Rob glanced back toward the house. "Vernon heard you banging on the window." He tossed his head in the direction of the rectangle of light coming from the basement. "He's the Helmes' son—a year younger than me. And that was Mr. Helmes who came to the door a minute ago."

"Oh, Rob—we're so lucky we found you!" Brittany said, hugging his arm.

"We were all set to go through every Hillam, Helman, and Heidelberg in the book!" added Cassie.

Rob looked at them in a kind of sideways glance that

Brittany knew meant he was reconsidering whether he wanted to join them or not.

"Oh, please, Rob—you've just got to come!" Brittany begged.

They heard the front door open just as a long shaft of light fell across the front lawn. "Who's out there?"

Rob pushed them back against the house and turned quickly toward the steps. "It's just some of the kids in the neighborhood—acting off," he mumbled, disappearing onto the porch. In a moment they heard the front door close.

It seemed like a long time, to Brittany, that they waited beside Lancelot under the shadows of a big tree, but Cassie, refusing to waste a single minute, made up a little rhyme to help them remember all the different things they needed to look for before they went back:

> *We must try to find everything*
> *Missing or lost,*
> *Like the plays by Ibsen*
> *And the poems by Frost;*
> *Candle, sugar,*
> *Shampoo, and soap—*
> *And even Uncle Anton's*
> *Stereoscope!*
> *And before we leave the neighborhood*
> *Of Bessie Montague,*
> *Find a jungle hat for Tiger*
> *And a beret for Brittany too!*

When Rob did return, it was from out of the shadows

around the back of the house—and, to Brittany's delight, he was carrying a rolled-up blanket and the small blue bag that he usually kept his gym clothes in. He looked nervous, and he almost jumped when he saw the stuffed parrot with the velvety moose antlers fanning out behind it.

"What on earth is that?" he scowled, leaning back.

"Lancelot," whispered Brittany proudly, "meet my brother Robert Bowers."

Rob swallowed, looking a little sick. "Wow...," he murmured. "I feel like I'm having some kind of a weird dream."

"If it's a dream, Robbie, you'll never want to wake up!" Brittany assured him. But he still looked doubtful as he walked to the garage, hesitating a couple of times and looking back over his shoulder. When he reappeared, he was mounted shakily on a somewhat faded ten-speed.

"Gosh," he said nervously, glancing back at the house. "I feel sort of creepy. I mean, I didn't even tell them I was going. I thought of trying to make up something—some excuse—but I finally just grabbed my stuff and sneaked out."

"Don't worry, Rob," Brittany urged. "It'll be okay. You'll be *so* glad you've come with us, I promise!"

"I can't believe this," he muttered uneasily. He glanced at Lancelot. "Do you both actually *ride* on that thing? No offense, but I think maybe you'd better come with me, Britt—okay? It'll be easier for me to pump you—

and, besides, there's an awfully lot of things you've got to explain—"

"Great!" Brittany said, giving Cassie a tight squeeze. "I'll tell him all about our cottage and Nicholas and Cow—"

"All aboard for Bessie Montague's!" Cassie said as she straddled Lancelot.

"—and your Uncle Anton and your twin brother Sebastian and about your shipwreck and how you can whisk us away to Kashmir and Zanzibar and—"

"I can't believe this," Rob said, smiling.

And the three of them wheeled off into the night.

Ashley and Tiger crouched in the tall grass, wishing they could shrivel up and disappear among the dark weeds and broken branches.

"What is it?" they heard the man by the headlights call out as the tall figure hovering above them grumbled a curse, as if in pain.

"I rammed into some fool thing here and 'bout ripped my gut open," he finally said. He seemed to stumble backwards, cursing under his breath. "There was a broken branch or something sticking up out of a log and it caught me right here between the ribs," they heard him telling the other one.

"Ouch," Tiger muttered painfully, sympathizing with the man in the shadows. Ashley too felt herself wince as she heard the man explaining his wound; yet she couldn't help feeling overwhelmingly relieved that his accidental collision with the sharp branch had saved them from being discovered.

There was a mumble from one of the men in the woods. Then: "Here, pour some of this on it." Silence. "Ouch—watch it! If there's anything left in there, I'd a lot rather have a swig of it than have it poured all down the front of my shirt." Laugh. "You always end up spilling half the bottle down the front of you, anyway, you dumb schmuck." Lots of mumbling. "Let's get out of here before I bleed to death." Laugh. "Lemme look in the light over here. All it did was tear your shirt. I'll bet it never even broke the skin." The voices faded off and then, after much slamming of car doors, the engine started up and the headlights withdrew down the lane as the car backed up and disappeared into total darkness.

Tiger broke into a soft whisper. "I was so scared," he said, hugging Nicholas tightly.

"Thank heavens they never found the cottage," Ashley exclaimed. She put her arm around Tiger and the two of them moved stealthily along the dark "path" until they found themselves at the back door.

Only a few coals remained glowing in the fireplace. Ashley lit a candle and then, to cheer them up, burnt part of a stick of jasmine incense.

"Close your eyes," she said, "and pretend we're in China . . . "

"You don't do it like Cassie does," Tiger complained.

"Well, give me a chance!"

But instead of playing the travel game just then, they finished off the rest of the cooked rhubarb, did the dishes, and then worked on their plays. Although Tiger immediately set to work on his, it was only when Ashley heard him calling his clown Pinocchio that the idea came to her to write a play about an eccentric dollmaker who had found she could make her creations come to life.

She wasn't sure how late it was when, after writing seven pages of her script, she finally looked over and saw Tiger, still clutching a puppet in each hand, asleep in the corner. For a moment she felt that maybe it was time for both of them to go to bed; but after she had tucked him under the quilt and then put a few more scraps of wood on the fire to take the night chill off the room, she felt alert enough that she determined to stick with her play until it was finished. And she almost did.

But later in the night, after she had written excitedly until her hand ached from holding the pencil, she began imagining sounds — sounds from the next room or outside the door or from up on the roof. For a long time, just the soft steady breathing coming from where Tiger and Nicholas lay curled up in the quilt was comforting enough; but now she jumped at every little clicking, creaking, or scratching noise she heard.

Just as she had finally assured herself that the sounds were made by birds and squirrels, something sent an icy ripple down her spine. Although she hadn't heard a car coming down the lane, the sudden dull thud followed by a man's voice and approaching footsteps paralyzed her with terror as she realized that the two men, for some reason, must have decided to come back and — this time — had discovered the cottage!

Do *something!* Ashley told herself. But the fear kept her frozen as the footsteps and muffled voices came nearer. *Run!* something commanded, but no sooner had her eyes shot toward the back way where they had fled a few hours earlier, than she spotted Tiger sleeping in the corner. Knowing she couldn't leave him there, she suddenly found the strength to leap up. Someone outside was fidgeting with the doorknob, she realized, and she quickly snatched up a big stick from the hearth and flattened herself against the wall behind the door just as it was thrown open.

"Ashley?" she heard Brittany's voice inquire meekly.

She felt all of strength leave her, and the heavy stick fell clattering to the floor.

Brittany jumped, and Rob and Cassie, too, fell back against the doorway, startled.

"Ashley!" Brittany gasped, catching her breath. Cassie immediately swept up the two of them in her arms, pulling them to her.

"We thought we heard you, love," Cassie said soothingly, while she smoothed her hand over the back of

Ashley's hair. "Just as we came to the door, we heard you scurrying around, but we never dreamed—"

"I was ready to bring that big stick down on the head of anyone who tried to get in here!" Ashley blurted out, trying her best not to cry. "I heard a man's voice"—and her eyes darted over to Rob as she caught her breath—"and I was positive that two drunk men had come back and were trying to break in—"

Cassie fished some broken bits of cookies out of a crumpled bag in her pocket and poked them into their mouths as if she were an old lady feeding pigeons in the park. For the next half hour they traded adventure stories, and Ashley tried to feel less shy around the fifteen-year-old boy she had only heard about. Mostly quiet while they recounted the evening's experiences, Rob seemed to be holding back, watching them with suspicion.

"—and so I couldn't get into the church this time, but I did rummage around Bessie's place until I came up with a few little tidbits," Cassie was saying. "But no hats, unfortunately," she added, casting a fond little glance toward Tiger who still lay sleeping in a ball under the quilt.

"What about the article!" Brittany suddenly burst forth, turning to Rob. "The one you told me about—the one about us—in the newspaper!"

Rob poked for a moment among the things in his gym bag. "Hey, Britt—there was more than one. There's been something in the local paper almost every night—and even a big write-up in the *Chronicle* yesterday — pictures and everything. You guys are notorious!" He pulled out a stack of newspaper clippings. "I think I saved everything. I mean — how did I know I was ever going to see you again?" For a moment he looked embarrassed, then he ducked his head and shuffled the clothes in his cloth bag.

Ashley and Brittany quickly spread out the newspaper articles on the floor while Cassie brought the candle and placed it among them.

"Look!" Brittany squealed. "It's us! How horrible — they used my old school picture and I've got one tooth missing!"

"Well, look at my hair!" gasped Ashley. "That's how I wore it in the fifth grade. I'll bet they got these pictures from the Child Protection Center. Tiger's the only one that looks half-way normal."

"Look what it says," said Cassie, running her finger under the heavy black lettering above the photographs: "'CHILDREN MISSING SINCE MONDAY FEARED KIDNAPPED.' Oh, be a sweet love, Ashley pie, and read it for us!"

Ashley swallowed and, by the light of the flickering candle, began to read:

> **CHESTERTON, Dayton County — Three foster children, missing since Monday evening when they left a Dayton County school bus, may have fallen victims of**

kidnappers, says Police Chief Rulon Hepworth of Fairmont. A statewide search has been conducted since Monday night when Frederick W. Oglethorpe, 314 Thistle Avenue, Chesterton, reported that the children had not returned from school.

Calvin Ridley, driver of the school bus, told police that he recalls that the children did not get off at the usual stop, but descended instead at the Wyler Bridge stop near the intersection of River Road and Highway 461.

Mrs. Oneida Finlayson, Paley's Crossing, reported Wednesday morning that three children matching the description released earlier by the police had been seen hitchhiking along Highway 461, two miles north of Chesterton, during Monday evening's thunderstorm. Mrs. Finlayson had given them a ride to a point eight or nine miles north of Chesterton, beyond the junction of Littlefield Road where the children told her they were invited to a birthday party. Mrs. Finlayson says she thought it was strange the children were unsure of the house and seemed to be carrying no gift.

Inquiries in that area have so far revealed nothing since none of the neighboring farms have children presently attending the Leavenworth Elementary School in Chesterton which the Oglethorpe foster children attended.

According to Chief Hepworth, the children may have accepted another ride from that point. Anyone having further

**information is urged to report immedi-
ately.**

"The *Oglethorpe* foster children —!" Ashley said, looking up. "As if we don't even have names of our own!"
She scanned the newspapers spread out on the floor and
began silently reading another article about them, while
Brittany and Cassie devoured still a third one. Suddenly
something caught her eye and she gasped. "Look! I think
it's about Lancelot!" Near the bottom of the page of one
of the papers was a small article which she excitedly began
reading aloud:

## Increase in Thefts Reported

**CHESTERTON, Dayton County — Ches-
terton police report an increase in minor
robberies since the Tuesday night break-
in of Fred and Irma's Bar and Grill. Ad-
ditional break-ins were also reported at
Huntley's Texaco on Center Street and at
the homes of J. J. Rigler, 820 West Haws
Avenue, and W. B. Moffit, at 18 West
Sumpter.**

**Still another break-in was reported to
have possibly occurred Tuesday night at
the First Baptist Church at Fifth and
O'Connor where vandals apparently ran-
sacked rummage-sale items.**

**The most bizarre of recent thefts con-
cerns a unique bicycle missing from a
private garage at 316 O'Connor. Leonard
Jacobsen, 29, owner of the vehicle, says
he had constructed it from parts of old
bicycles and decorated it with such di-**

**verse items as an Italian tapestry, moose
antlers, and a stuffed parrot.
According to Jacobson, the unique cycle
was intended for use in this year's an-
nual 4th of July parade where, for the
past four years, Jacobson has taken part
as a clown. A reward is offered.**

Rob was staring at Cassie in unbelief. "You *stole*
that?"

"How much do you think the reward would be if we
took it back?" Brittany asked excitedly.

"Brittany!" Rob scolded. "That thing's stolen. You
guys can't just walk off with something and then take it
back and expect a reward!"

Ashley suddenly turned to Cassie: "What I want to
know is—" She hesitated, swallowed, then went on: "I
mean—did you break into *all* of those places?"

Cassie looked bewildered, then hurt. She reached up,
almost absentmindedly, pulled a long lock of her silvery
hair from beneath the little felt hat, and wound it slowly
around her finger. Then, while all the eyes in the room
continued to focus on her, she looked at them and spoke
softly: "My dears, my sweet little dears—for what possible reason in the world would Cassandra du Maurier
break into the Texaco service station?"

"What about the Bar and Grill or whatever it was—
and those people's houses?" Brittany felt brave enough
to ask.

Cassie seemed to be gathering herself together as

she gave a deep sigh and then smiled as elegantly and gently and warmly as if she were a Southern hostess welcoming long-lost relatives to her plantation on Christmas Eve. "Gracious me, little dumplings—cross my heart and hope to die—I'm pure. I never took anything from any of *those* places."

"But what about—" the three of them all seemed to say at once.

"Wait!" Cassie cautioned gently, still smiling as she held up one finger to stop their chatter. "I did go to Bessie Montague's—three different times, I think—and I got my watercolor paper and some of the things I'd left in her closet—one of which, by the way, I'm just *dying* to show you! Anyway, I may have borrowed a thing or two from Bessie—a little sugar here, a little cinnamon there—but, of course, I'll return it eventually—and more! And I *did* go into the church once or twice—and took, as I told you, many of the clothes—some of these lovely things we're wearing, in fact—that I myself had given them for a rummage sale long, long, *long* ago," she said, waving her hand in the air with a flourish.

"Even *these?*" Brittany asked, touching the oatmeal sweater and cinnamon-colored knickers she had borrowed from Tiger to wear into town.

Again Cassie waved a single finger. "No, no, no. Those I simply borrowed from the rummage sale they never seem to get around to having. They were donated, after all," she continued, "to clothe the needy—and who, pray tell, is needier than my little baby birds that I left chirping here in our little Crumbledown nest?"

"But what about that—that thing out there?" Rob asked somewhat grumpily. "Lancelot or whatever you call it. I suppose you think of *that* as some kind of donation too—!"

Brittany winced at how loud his voice had become, and she squeezed in closer to Cassie and hugged her arm. Why was he being so mean? Rob—of all people—who had even stolen a couple of things himself!

"Lancelot," Cassie went on soothingly, "*chose* to come."

"*Chose*—" Rob started to say.

"I was simply passing by a dark cavern," Cassie went on, "a sort of deep grotto—"

"How about just a plain simple *garage*," Rob said, sarcastically.

"Whatever," Casie trilled, unflustered. "Cavern, grotto, garage—something, at any rate, incredibly dark and mysterious." Rob rolled his eyes, and Cassie went on.

"And—all of a sudden—something seems to whisper, 'Come on, Cassie—let's fly!' "

"Good grief," Rob mumbled, and Ashley scowled at him.

"And we did!" Cassie said happily. "We flew—together! Oh, he'll go back. He certainly must go back. But, for the time being—"

"For the time being," Rob butted in, "for the time being, lady, the whole state police force is looking everywhere for Brittany and these guys. And when they catch all of you here with stolen goods—"

"But who, my child, is going to tell them where we are?" Cassie asked, reaching out one finger to touch Rob lightly on the chest. "Are *you?*"

Rob stalled, and Brittany saw him swallow.

"You can't stay here forever," he said firmly.

"Maybe not," Cassie said very softly. "But we'll stay just as long as we possibly can. We'll stretch our days, our hours, our minutes, just as long as we can possibly stretch them. And we'll fill each moment with wonders and marvels until it's ready to burst. But no one, dear Robino—*no* one will *ever* say we didn't *live!*"

Rob was silent. Cassie's finger still touched his chest, and on each side of her, Ashley and Brittany snuggled in closer. Suddenly she gave a deep sigh, breaking the silence, and then, with a flick of her wrist that almost seemed to the girls to spread glittering fairy dust around the room, she whispered: "Quick! Scat! All of you! To bed—before you turn into little white mice!"

Rob stood, without moving, staring at her.

"You too, *m'sieur*," she whispered. And as he started to speak, she put a finger to her lips. "No more words tonight, please. There are little night demons who can appear from nowhere after midnight to twist our words and warp our thoughts. Wait, please—wait until morning and see how different everything will seem. Bombs bursting all around us at midnight can be transformed, in the clear light of day, into nothing more than delicate little bubbles vanishing into the air."

"But—"

"Please, little dove. Please," she whispered even more softly. "Trust the morning."

# 17

And Cassie was right: things *did* seem brighter and happier in the morning.

Whether it was the sweet scent of pine needles or simply the sunlight filtering through the uncovered window that awakened her, Ashley wasn't sure. But she sat up suddenly, saw Nicholas stretching himself in the rays of warm morning light, and heard Brittany, beside her, yawn heartily.

She rolled over. "Brit," she asked, poking the figure that had squirmed down under the cover. "Where's Cassie?"

The top of Brittany's head emerged from under the blanket, followed by two bright eyes. Suddenly she raised herself up on one elbow. The door to Cassie's little room was ajar and only the big coat with the fur collar lay rumpled across the sagging cot.

"I don't know," Brittany said, pulling herself up and looking around. "I just barely woke up."

"I wonder what time it is," Ashley pondered.

A rustling noise outside startled her, and she looked up to see the door opening and Cassie, showing no traces of having been up half the night, swooping in loaded with fragrant lilacs that matched the long filmy lavender gown she wore.

"*Bonjour!*" she twittered radiantly. "*Bonjour, mes petits!* Look what I found over by the edge of one of the fields!" She swirled about the room depositing clusters of the perfumed flowers in every bottle or jug. "Our milk has been cooling in the stream since daybreak, and I've peeled the boiled eggs so they're ready to eat. We can mash them or just sprinkle salt and pepper on them and—"

Tiger stirred and then sat up abruptly. "You found him! You found Brittany's brother!"

"But, of course, little prince!" Cassie trilled. "We couldn't come home empty-handed, could we? If we hadn't managed to find young Robin Hood here, we'd have been obliged, I'm afraid, to bring home some gypsy child! But, yes, little Tigedore—we found the long-lost brother!"

"Just like you found *your* long-lost twin brother that time!" said Tiger.

Rob rolled over on his back, stretching, then he peered at them upside down. "What's this about a twin brother?"

"That's what I was going to tell you about on the way home last night," Brittany told him, "only we never got that far."

Rob mumbled something grumpily and rolled back over on his stomach, burying his face in his folded arms.

Just then, waving a stick of smoking incense like a magic wand, Cassie swirled into the center of the room, her lavender skirts swishing. "Well, my little ginger-snaps — where will it be this morning? Can you guess?"

Ashley closed her eyes and breathed deeply. That was it! The taunting scent that had wrapped itself around her and almost lifted her from her bed when she had first awakened: the fresh yet musty-sweet smell of deep-green pine needles. She lay back on her quilt and closed her eyes as Cassie's voice crooned of pine forests sprinkled with powdered-sugar snow; of crackling fires and bala-laikas; of rosy-cheeked Ivans and Natashas, bundled in furs, huddled in the decorated sleds drawn by three horses that almost flew through the white-birch woods.

"It's winter," Cassie breathed, "and the sparkling Snow Maiden has just appeared in the forest where the old peasant couple had fashioned her out of snowflakes and ice . . . "

Ashley opened her eyes long enough to verify that they were still in a lilac-strewn cottage on a spring morning, then, noticing that Cassie's magic seemed to have made even Rob — as well as Brittany and Tiger — sink back onto the covers and daydream, she let her eyes fall shut again and felt herself almost floating over snow-dusted forests of fir where crystal lakes and silver-ribbon streams glistened and glittered among the deep green and dazzling white.

Cassie's soothing voice had taken on a faint Russian

accent now as she went on unfolding the rich details of her wintry tale. Ashley let herself drift, remembering how snowflakes had felt on her cheeks and nose and tongue the two or thee times she had actually seen a real snow-fall . . .

A muffled voice broke through the whirl of snow: "And miles to go before I sleep, and miles to go before I sleep . . . " It was Cassie. "That's Robert Frost," she heard Cassie's voice go on to say, and Ashley plummeted back to the reality of Crumbledown with its strange mixture of pine and lilac smells. She sat up, looking around. The door to the cottage was open. And Rob was gone.

"Well," Cassie announced with a sigh. "Enough of frosts and blizzards!" And she waved the pine incense dramatically as if to dismiss the last snowflake from their minds. "It's spring, my dears — and we mustn't waste one little tidbit of it! Up, up!" she coaxed in her flute-like voice, swirling herself to her feet. "Let's have a nibble of breakfast, then see what the morning has brought us!"

While Brittany and Tiger leaped up and started tidying up the rumpled covers on their grass beds, Ashley slipped over to the open door and peeked out. A few yards away, Rob squatted under one of the trees, pulling nervously at clumps of grass and then ripping the blades into little shreds.

Ashley only hesitated a moment then found herself going over to him. "What's the matter?" she asked. "What are you doing?"

He looked up and stared at her sulkily. "Nothing, really," he mumbled finally. Then: "I just can't figure that old lady out. She's got to be the weirdest—"

"Cassie?" Ashley interrupted. "You don't like Cassie? Oh, wait until you know her! There's no one in the whole world like Cas—"

"You're telling me!" Rob broke in. "Doesn't she bug you with all those phony accents and—"

"They're not phony!" Ashley replied quickly, defending her. "I mean—of course she's got lots of accents. She's a very famous actress—Cassandra du Maurier!"

"You bet she's an actress! I can't believe all the garbage she's filled you guys with—like all this stuff Brittany was telling me last night about being the missing daughter of Czar Nicholas and—"

"She only told us she *might* be. Even Cassie admits she's not really sure! But she has been all over the world and knows lots of dukes and counts and—"

"She's out of her mind," Rob blurted out. "There are people, you know, who can tell you things—almost anything—in such a way that—well, they sort of hypnotize you and brainwash you until you end up believing anything they say."

Ashley felt a little shivering sensation on the back of her neck. "Do you—do you think Cassie's—evil?"

"Well—maybe not evil, exactly. But she's got to be crazy!"

Ashley wanted to say something but nothing would

come out. She only felt an uncomfortable ache growing inside her. And when she finally did speak, the words almost gushed out in a stream of emotion.

"If you only knew how terrified we were the first night when we woke up and found her poking at us like some old witch! But then—then we began to see how she really is. And—and she became so beautiful—*so* beautiful—and so good!" Ashley dropped to her knees beside Rob. "She really *might* be magic, you know. Don't ask me how it works, but she can pick up the ugliest rock or stick or—or anything—and suddenly she has you believing that it's the most fabulous and beautiful thing you've seen in your whole life!"

"That's what I mean! She's even got you guys believing it's all right to break in a house and just take anything that—"

"Oh, no—you'll see. She only goes back to Bessie Montague's because she used to stay there and that's where she's stored a lot of her things. And besides—even the place where we get our milk—we have to pay them back some way. We'll figure out a way to make cupcakes or brownies or—" She stopped abruptly as something tumbled through her mind. For a second she hesitated, then found herself daring to say it: "Didn't *you* ever take anything in your life?"

Rob looked at her. Feeling uncomfortable, she still went on: "Brittany told me once that—that her brother had gotten into trouble—for shoplifting."

She wasn't sure if he blinked or not, but suddenly she heard him answering; "So what if I did? Does that make it all right?" He looked down and brushed something off his shoe. "I stole some things last year—just little things—like candy bars and comic books and stuff. But I don't want Brittany and you guys doing anything like that." Again, he fumbled around with his shoe. "It seems sort of dumb to me now—and I'm sorry I did it."

Ashley found herself feeling warm. After a few seconds of silence, she heard herself announce: "I've got it! Maybe it would make you feel better if you helped us when we pay back the farmer for the milk—and for the eggs. Maybe we can—"

They could suddenly hear Cassie singing and looked up to see her flitting back and forth in front of the cottage, straightening a drooping hollyhock here, snipping off a straggling vine there.

"If you only knew what she's been through," Ashley said sympathetically as Cassie continued to busy herself with trimming the ivy around the doors and windows. "She really might be the princess Anastasia, you know, who had to escape from Russia when the—"

"Come on," Rob interrupted. "I've heard all that from Britt—and I don't believe a word of it." He looked down at the ground disgustedly. Suddenly he looked up. "And what's all this about a shipwreck?"

Ashley glanced back at the cottage where Cassie occupied herself with removing the weeds that grew around the doorstep. "I wish you could hear Cassie tell it her-self—but I think it was when they were fleeing from Russia—and she and her twin brother got shipwrecked. I think she thought he was drowned or something, but anyway, she ended up alone on this island with his clothes and for a long time—I'm not sure how long—but anyway she had to dress up like a boy and—"

She stopped. Rob was staring at her strangely.

"What's wrong?"

"Don't tell me she got hired as a messenger for a duke and—"

"She did!" Ashley exclaimed. Then, trying to keep her voice low, she went on: "But how did *you* know?"

"Are you kidding me? She said she worked for a duke?"

"I think—and the funny thing was, the duke sent her to deliver all these love messages to his girlfriend—and, because he thought Cassie was a boy, she—"

"Oh, no," Rob groaned. "I can't believe it." He looked at Ashley. "Don't tell me the lady's name was Olivia—and the twin brother's name was—"

"Sebastian," Ashley said, puzzled. "Why? Did Brittany already tell you all this?"

"Sebastian!" Again Rob groaned. "No, Brittany didn't tell me. Do you know that we studied all of this in English last year?"

"About *Cassie?*" Ashley gasped.

"About Shakespeare!" Rob echoed back emphatically. "Did she tell you all this happened to *her?*"

"Well," Ashley began, "she said that—"

"Do you know that Shakespeare wrote that? It's the play of *Twelfth Night!*"

For a moment Ashley stared at him. "It is?" she finally heard herself say. She felt sick.

"She's taken a story from Shakespeare," Rob went on, "and made you guys think that—"

"Ssh!" Ashley warned. "Here she comes!"

Cassie sailed across the grass in a ripple of lavender. "There you are!" she trilled, stopping in front of Rob and Ashley where they sat in the shade. "Ooooh! Don't move—not a tittle, not a tad. I'd love to frame you just how you are—two exquisitely beautiful young people with skin looking like peaches and cream and your hair stealing sparkles from the morning sun! Now who would suspect—with those apricot cheeks—that you haven't yet eaten your breakfast! Come! We'll take our eggs and watercress down to the grassy bank where the milk is cooling in the stream. Isn't it simply glorious?" she sang out, whirling around and looking up at the clear blue sky.

And it did turn out glorious, somehow. Even though several times throughout the day Ashley would catch herself remembering uneasily what Rob had told her about Cassie's borrowing of the story from *Twelfth Night,* it still turned out to be another day that she wanted to remember forever.

Topping off their breakfast with fresh crimson berries, they ran along the edge of the brook, following it upstream through trees and meadows to where it came gurgling down between the hills, and, still further up, tumbling down through a narrow rocky gorge where the foliage hung thick and green overhead. There they played a game of colors — each of them secretly choosing a certain hue and shade and then acting out in pantomime or dance the way it made them feel until the others could guess the color. For most of the game, Rob sat back against a tree, watching suspiciously and reluctantly; but when, near the end, Cassie did an elaborate interpretation that sent her leaping over logs and waving her arms in sudden bursts and explosions, it was Rob who guessed that she was giving her interpretation of the color red-orange. He didn't participate when Cassie taught them a Japanese song about cherry blossoms and then a Russian one about a birch tree, but later when they acted out scenes from famous paintings, he did finally consent to be one of the survivors on *The Raft of the Medusa*.

They all made stick boats with leaf sails to race along the stream as they made their way home, and then they sat in the shade at noon-time and watched Tiger's puppet show — a lively production about a boy name Pinocchio who went to take cookies to his grandmother and stumbled onto a candy house in the woods. When at last the show was over, Tiger begged Rob to go with him to the stream to look for the best places to fish. Cassie and Brittany then scampered off with their watercolors, leaving Ashley for more than two hours to finish her play.

The rest of the afternoon was spent rehearsing in the trees. More than once Cassie exclaimed how "positively brilliantly written" the play was, and even Rob finally agreed, although reluctantly, to do the part Ashley had written for him. But he went back sulking even more when, after the rehearsal, Cassie offered to teach them all to weave.

"What we need," Cassie said, "is a loom of some kind." She looked at Rob. "And I'm sure—after seeing the wonderful fishing pole you made this afternoon for little Tigedore—that you are just clever enough to think of something fabulous! Our tools may be a wee bit crude," she added, "but you're ingenious enough that you're bound to come with something marvelous—I just know it!"

The muscles in Rob's jaw seemed to twitch just a little, and Ashley also thought she noticed a slight squirm before he rolled over on his stomach on the grass and lay, without saying a word, his cheek resting on his folded arms.

"Well, my little pigeons," Cassie announced with a sigh. "Time to fly back to Crumbledown."

"And will you show us the surprise you said you got at Bessie Montague's?" Brittany asked.

"Glory forevermore!" Cassie exclaimed. "I almost forgot! Come—we'll make a spectacular fire now that darkness is creeping in on us, and then I'll show you something positively wonderful—something left me years and years ago by my Uncle Anton."

After they had blocked out the windows at the cottage

and started a fire, Cassie disappeared into her little room, and for a few minutes they could hear her rummaging in the dark among her collection of shopping bags. In a moment she appeared, unwrapping from under a large purple scarf something dark and angular.

She held it up—a pair of black tubes linked together like binoculars and attached to a sliding metal frame. In silent awe the children leaned over and watched her unwrap a tall stack of long cards, each one bearing two identical photographs. Even Rob sat up and watched with interest as she picked up the top card and slipped it carefully into the metal frame. Cassie peeked in, adjusted the frame and then beamed as she handed it to Tiger.

"Look at that!" she whispered. "The pyramids of Egypt!"

Tiger's eyes widened. "Oh, my gosh!" he gasped. "It's real!"

"It's a stereopticon," Cassie proudly announced.

Eager for her turn, Brittany put her head close to Tiger's, straining to steal a peek through a corner of the large black metal tubes. "Can I see?" she begged. And she too gasped when she took them in her own hands and peered into the dark tunnels at the twin pictures beyond. "The camel—it's almost coming right out of the picture!" Staring at the camel and pyramids, so real before her eyes, Brittany thought of what Ashley had told her about Cassie probably not really even having a twin brother named Sebastian at all. She still wanted to believe it—even if Shakespeare *had* written a story that was awfully similar. But she knew with all her heart that Cassie had at least traveled all around the world and seen all of these places and knew everything about them.

When it was Ashley's turn she could hardly believe her eyes. The identical pictures of Egypt merged into one remarkable scene in which the pyramids, palm tree, and camel all stood out three-dimensionally against the background.

"Can we see another one?" Tiger pleaded, while Rob was taking his turn with the strange apparatus.

"Why, you may see them all—in good time, my little man," Cassie told him. "But wouldn't it be more special if we limited ourselves to maybe five or six pictures each evening—carefully studying each wonderful little detail and savoring it fully? Wouldn't that be a delicious treat to look forward to?"

She gently picked up a second card and slipped it delicately into the metal frame. Ashley craned her neck enough to discover that this time the two black-and-white photographs pictured an eskimo family arranged outside their igloo. Taking turns, the five of them traded gasps and giggles and even moments of spellbound silence as they toured Kenya, Honduras, Nova Scotia, and Lapland by way of the enchanting double images that magically blended into miniature scenes so dazzlingly real it made their heads spin.

"Can I please see the one with the elephant and the banana trees again?" Tiger persuaded.

"Of course, my *petit*," Cassie said. "And don't forget to smell the mangoes and guavas and papayas this time — listen for the monkeys and parrots chattering among the vines!" And just as her eyes were beginning to drift shut, suddenly they popped open, lively and dark. "And while you men are chasing zebras in Kenya or herding reindeer in Norway, perhaps we three beauties might slip down to the stream and take our evening bath. What do you say, my little water nymphs?"

"Great!" Brittany squeaked. "But can I look at all the pictures again when we come back?"

"Over and over!" Cassie reassured her. And quickly they gathered up their things and hurried out into the dusky light.

Tiger carefully removed the picture of Nova Scotia fishermen and replaced it with the jungles of Honduras again. Rob leaned back, resting on his elbows; then, spotting the stack of unseen photocards only partly covered by the purple scarf protecting them, he inched over and stole a peek at the half-protruding photograph on top.

"Hey," he whispered. "What do you say me and you sneak a little preview of up-coming attractions, Colonel Williamsboo?"

Tiger lowered the stereopticon. "Colonel what? How come you called me that?"

"Well, that's what it says on your T-shirt: Colonel Williamsboo!"

Tiger pulled his chin in against his chest and tried to peer down the front of his shirt at the blue letters spread across in an arch. "No, it doesn't. Ashley told me it says 'Williamsburg' or something like that — doesn't it?"

"Maybe once upon a time — but not now, punk. See all those blank spaces?" Rob asked. And he pointed how the letters missing from COLONIAL WILLIAMSBURG now left only COLON AL WILLIAMSBU. "So that's what you'll have to be, I'm afraid — Colonel Williamsboo. But that's a whole lot better than being just a common old PFC or Corporal or something, isn't it? After all, you're probably in command — leader of the regiment. You *are* in charge here, aren't you?"

Tiger blushed and beamed, not quite sure how to handle what he was hearing. "Well, I'm not the boss of *everything*," he said, squirming until his neck almost disappeared between his shoulders. "But I *am* the puppet master. Cassie said!"

"Well, then, Colonel — how about it? Do we get to steal a peek at tomorrow's big offering?" Rob reached out two fingers and temptingly lifted up the corner of the top picture on the big stack. "What do you say?"

Again, Tiger shrugged uncomfortably. "I dunno. I guess. But only the top one," he added quickly, "or maybe Cassie'll get —"

"Hey —" Rob said, cutting him off, "you'll like this

one. It even looks like your friend Nicholas the Cat over there."

Tiger stretched his neck to see the new card with two identical pictures that Rob was slipping into the metal frame. Rob looked in, adjusted the focus, then turned it over to Tiger. "How's that one? Pretty neat, huh?"

Tiger turned his back so that the light from the fire brightly illuminated the new scene in the stereopticon. It was wonderful: on the deck of a ship, a little girl with her cat sat perched amazingly lifelike atop a gigantic coil of rope while the wind blew her hair that hung down from beneath her dark beret.

Tiger's eyes lingered fondly, lovingly, on each detail, the way Cassie had suggested. He didn't want to let this picture go. In fact, of all the exciting and interesting pictures they had seen this evening, this, he decided was his favorite. And it was almost as if — somewhere — he had seen it before.

The door burst open and Ashley charged in. "We forgot the shampoo," she sighed, out of breath. "Cassie brought us some shampoo back from —"

"Look!" Tiger blurted out. "The best one yet! Look how real —"

Rob grabbed his arm and was about to say "Ssh," but Ashley had already turned around and was bending down to take the stereopticon from his hands.

"She won't tell," Tiger was saying, "And besides, I

don't think Cassie will really mind as long as we just look—"

But Ashley was not listening. Adjusting the sliding metal frame to refocus the picture, she felt a little shiver zigzag down her spine. "It's Cassie," she breathed. "It's a picture of her—of Anastasia—when she was a little girl—probably coming to America for the first time—or when she fled to Poland or wherever it was—"

Rob stood up and seemed to be squinting his eyes to look at something on the back of the card.

"This can't be Cassie. No way. These pictures, you gotta remember, are something you used to be able to buy in a store. Besides, look!" And he pulled the card from the frame and turned it over, bending down by the fire so that they both could read it:

KEYSTONE VIEW PUBLISHERS
COPYRIGHTED
MADE IN USA
Mariangela and Her Cat Pasquale Sail
to Sardinia

"See—it's just something she must have bought—or maybe even her father or grandfather bought. I don't know—it's real old, anyway," Rob said. "What made you think it was Cassie? Did *she* tell you that?"

Ashley stared into the fire, trying to bring back the shreds of a memory that flapped and fluttered in her mind like tattered laundry.

"No . . . not exactly. It was just something she said,"

Ashley mumbled. "Something about going around the world with her Uncle Anton." She paused, then went on, her eyes narrowing as she strained to recall the fragments: "She told us how she sat on a coil of rope on the deck of the ship, wearing her little beret and holding her pet cat . . . "

"She must have dreamed that up from this picture," Rob announced, his voice making Ashley shiver. "I'll bet she never went around the world at all!"

*Never even went around the world at all.* The idea made Ashley feel cold even though the long flames from the fire continued to quiver upwards, heating her cheeks.

"But she must have been to Vienna at least," she tired to tell herself, speaking aloud. "And Kashmir and—" She stopped. How could it not all be true? If it was all a lie, then—"

Tiger was on his feet tugging at Ashley's hand. "She went! She really went, Ashley—I just know she did!"

"And we all went too," Ashley's voice seemed to say, though it sounded very very far away.

Rob found himself twisting and turning throughout most of the night. Who *was* this woman who lived in an abandoned house at the edge of the woods and wove such an incredible fabric of stories around her that she caught up everyone within listening distance into her magic spell?

Could there be any truth at all in the tales she told about being the heiress Anastasia, descendant of the Russian Czar? About having been a famous actress on the stages of Europe? About traveling to all the far-off corners of the world with her uncle?

Again, he squirmed and shifted in his makeshift bed. And when it felt as if it surely must be morning, he raised himself up on one elbow, pulled aside the crooked piece of plywood covering the window, and peeked out through the lace and chenille curtains. It was still not quite daybreak, yet he knew he was too restless to lie in bed any longer. Slipping out as quietly as he could, he quickly dressed, then carefully let himself out through the crooked door with the broken hinge. *I guess I ought to try to fix that door,* he caught himself thinking, but then added quickly, *—that is, if I really plan on sticking around.*

What must the Helmeses be thinking? It was hard to

imagine he'd only been gone a little more than twenty-four hours—but surely they had notified the police by now. They weren't a bad family, the Helmeses. Not very exciting maybe, but, still, not bad, all in all. Too bad Brittany had not been as lucky.

He realized he was wandering now along the rough little path that ran beside the stream until it led him through the trees and up between the hills where the water spilled down through the rocky crevice where Cassie and the kids had acted out their color-guessing game the day before.

If he took his bike and went back now, he would have to take Brittany with him. And yet—that was the problem. If the Oglethorpes were even half as bad as Brittany and Ashley claimed, there was no way he could make her go back there.

But if he couldn't take Brittany back, he wasn't about to leave *without* her either. What was the answer? Each time Brittany came into his mind now, it was the bright-eyed smiling girl, almost ready to burst with excitement, that had come with Cassie on that impossible bicycle to find him at Chesterton.

It was not the same girl he had visited in the schoolyard last winter, not even the same little sister he'd lived with at the Millers' or the frightened little girl he'd tried to shelter in their own home during those turbulent months when their mother had been wasting away and Harold was taken off to prison. The Brittany he couldn't

shake now from his mind was the pretty girl he had
watched yesterday dancing out the colors amber and tur-
quoise or eagerly memorizing every syllable of the Japanese folk song Cassie had begun to teach them.

Cassandra du Maurier. The name tumbled around in
his mind. It was all too bizarre. Maybe she had never
been in a shipwreck of her own—maybe had never even
sailed on a ship at all—but she had someway rescued
Brittany from a disaster of a different kind. She seemed,
in fact, to be working her magic in such a way that she
was saving them all—Brittany, Ashley, Tiger, and maybe
even himself. Saving them from what? From the families
they didn't like? From themselves? He wasn't sure, but
he knew that, after barely a day with her, he would never
again be quite the same. Still—

He found himself hurrying back alongside the stream
down the damp and rocky path toward Crumbledown.

The rest of that day and the two days following were,
for Rob, like some wild and endless carnival ride. The
whole thing made him feel disoriented and dizzy. Jolted
first this way and that, he felt as if he were barely able
to hang on while the little car speeding him along some
unfamiliar track continually jerked him from one way of
thinking to another.

If Cassie had really concocted for herself some fantastical past—some stories borrowed, others entirely
made-up—she was still, he had to admit, the most thrilling

and imaginative storyteller he had ever heard. And the problem was, some of her strange tales, he felt, *were* true. He just wasn't always sure where to draw the line. But one thing *was* certain: if life at the Helmeses had been rather monotonous and dull, each hour of every day here at Crumbledown seemed to be bursting with new surprises.

By the afternoon of his fourth day, he had milked his first cow, caught more fish than he could count, designed and built a rabbit trap and the beginnings of a loom, devised three new puppets for Tiger, and constructed an open-air theater stage in the trees behind the house. But that wasn't all: he had become converted to rhubarb yogurt, feasted on fried trout with mint leaves and roast rabbit with mushrooms, and learned to cook a soufflé. And even more: he had fallen in love with the poems of Robert Frost, learned more French, German, and Spanish than he had ever thought possible, resolved to find out more about Leonardo da Vinci, Herman Melville, and Wolfgang Amadeus Mozart; learned a Swiss yodeling song and a Maori war chant; and made up his mind to take accordion lessons from Cassie as soon as she could locate where her Rumanian instrument had been stored.

By Friday afternoon — at least he thought it was Friday afternoon, although he had to admit that the names of the days of the week had become less important at Crumbledown — he had a list in his notebook two and a half pages long under the heading THINGS I WANT TO DO:

NOW AND IN THE FUTURE. He had just left Tiger watching some baby hummingbirds discovered in a nest in the eaves of the cottage, when he came upon Brittany and Ashley taking turns with the watercolors as they sat in the shade near where Lancelot was parked.

"Colonel Boo is trying to figure out a way to work a chorus line of hummingbirds into his next show," he told them, smiling. "Where's Cassie?"

Ashley went on coloring, tipping her head to one side as she studied the particular shade of bluish-gray she had just let flow into the rich olive color next to it.

"I think she's memorizing her part for the play," Brittany responded without looking up.

Rob quietly studied their efforts to capture Crumble-down in watercolor, almost wishing he were doing it too, then said: "It's too bad we can't really have an audience. For the play, I mean."

Brittany looked up, without saying anything, then announced suddenly: "Do you think there's any way we could invite the family over that owns Cow? I mean, we haven't taken them anything yet and maybe —"

"No way!" Rob and Ashley piped at the same time. "I mean, it *would* be great," Rob added. "It's just that they'd probably figure out in a minute who we are and then it would all be over."

"Do you think they're *still* looking for us?" Brittany asked.

"The police? No question. But I'm pretty sure that

by now they must think we've even gone to another state," Rob said. "Imagine if they knew we were all still just a few miles from Chesterton!"

"Has anyone added up how long we've been gone?" Ashley asked, running the corner of her brush along the paper where a blob of coral-color seemed to be gathering to run.

"Four days for me, I think," Rob answered. "And I guess that means about seven or eight for you guys."

Brittany looked up, open-mouthed. "Only seven or eight days?"

Rob knew exactly what she was thinking. Every day had become so full, so rich, that it seemed as if a lifetime had been crowded into what was, for him, not even a week. And yet, nothing had dragged. The whole time, in a way, had seemed infinitely shorter than one hour in the civics class he had from Mr. Cartwright.

Just then Cassie's voice, dramatic yet tuneful, drifted through the trees as she rehearsed her role as the eccentric dollmaker.

Rob shook his head. "Wow—! If we could only get into our parts the way Cassie does—!"

"Cassie promised to help me with mine tonight," Brittany said. "In fact, she says maybe we could all have a half-an-hour acting class every morning if we wanted."

Rob felt an unexpected little surge of anticipation. Even if Cassie were not a lost Russian princess—and if she had never been shipwrecked with a twin brother named Sebastian or sailed around the world with her rich Uncle Anton—at least there was no question that she *was* an actress. And maybe she *had* been famous in her day. It was possible, at least.

His eye caught Ashley's just as he glanced up momentarily from her watercoloring. "Did you—did you ever ask her about the stereopticon picture?" he asked.

Ashley shook her head, dipping her brush into a little pool of raw umber. "I didn't. I just—I just couldn't," she said.

"Maybe the little girl with the cat *is* her," Brittany put in earnestly. "How do *we* know what she looked like when she was escaping from Russia?"

Rob shook his head. "No. It's printed right on the stereopticon picture that it's some Italian girl on a boat headed for a place called Sardinia."

"Well, there's always the chance that it's just a coincidence," Ashley reasoned. "I mean, there must have been lots of little girls wearing berets and holding cats on sailing ships back in those—"

"I guess there's even a bigger chance," Rob cut in, "that she used to sit with her Uncle Anton or whoever he was and look at all those pictures from around the world until she started believing she had actually done all those things and visited all those places . . ."

"But does it even *matter?*" Brittany blurted out.

And Rob knew that, somehow, it probably *didn't* matter—that somehow—

Cassie's voice interrupted them as she came swishing and swirling through the trees, dressed in her artichoke costume accented by various gold and emerald scarves. "Trying to catch hold of this glorious afternoon forever?" She spotted the girls' almost-finished paintings and clasped her hands in delight. "Oooh, how perfectly splendid!" she crooned, as one hand fluttered up to her forehead and she turned her head away as though completely overcome by their talents. "Such beauty makes me positively dizzy," she confessed, dramatically. "And yours — dear Robino — where's *your* interpretation of Crumbledown?"

"In my head, I guess," he smiled.

"But you must *share* it, love!" Cassie's voice rang out. "How else are we going to know all the lovely and wonderful things the way *you* saw them?"

Feeling as though he must be blushing, Rob looked down as his shoe nudged persistently at a stubborn root. "I'm afraid I'd make a terrible artist," he said.

"Why, only if you think there is just *one* right way to capture such a thing on paper," Cassie explained. "That's the glory of an artist," she went on, " — to offer us a fresh *new* way of seeing things. Goodness me, the poorest little camera in the world could take a snapshot in a second and capture what the eye sees and we'd never ever have need of another artist again."

"Well, then —" Ashley started to say.

"Ah," Cassie interrupted, "but that's the marvel: for the true artist doesn't just copy nature — he recreates it!"

Cassie reached down and picked up the brush that wasn't being used and put it in Rob's hand. "That's why, you see, we must have a chance to share *your* vision of this wonderful little cottage — for no one else in the world, dear Robino, would ever paint it quite the same as you!"

"But Cassie," Brittany started, "I don't get it. Is it really true that we are all seeing something different when we look at Crumbledown?"

"Well, yes and no, little buttercup. I'm quite certain we all see that it's a cottage on the edge of the woods. But some people will notice the soft outlines of the surrounding greenery — and someone else will notice the sharp angles in the roof. Someone will emphasize the lavender qualities in the shadows, while someone else will focus on the luscious greenness of the ivy."

"But how about the people that paint modern art?" Rob put in. "I hate it when you can't even tell —"

"Oh, hate — no, no, not hate, Robbie dear. We must never say hate," Cassie said. Then she went on: "Do you know what that means?"

All three of the children were looking at her now. "It means, dear loves, that we simply don't understand. Whenever we say something is ugly, we are usually admitting that we just don't know enough about it. And it's amazing, my sweets, what happens when we take the time to learn a little bit and become more familiar — for what we thought was ugliness begins to disappear and beauty grows in its place."

*It's true,* Rob thought. *It is so true—not just of things like modern art, but of people as well.* He found himself studying Cassie's eyes, gleaming and sparkling as she talked, and noticing how the afternoon light, coming from behind, illuminated her long hair with an otherworldly silver glow. It was the transformation Ashley had told him about, and though he suspected it had been taking place little by little over the last four days, he knew, without a doubt, it was happening now with an almost overwhelming power.

"Let Robbie borrow a sheet from your pad, please, Poppyseed," Cassie was saying to Brittany, "and we'll let him open our eyes just a little wider by helping us to see what only *he* perhaps can see in dear, dear Crumbledown."

"And then you must do one too, Cassie—and Tiger too!" insisted Ashley.

"Oh, *bien sur, mes petits!* Absolutely! And then we'll have a wonderful art show and display them all—*not,* remember, to see which one is *best,* but to simply relish the variety, my loves—and just enjoy all the different and fascinating interpretations."

Nervously holding the brush Cassie had given him, Rob took the clean sheet of thick, rough paper offered by Brittany and situated himself in a shady spot within reach of the set of glistening watercolors.

"Here goes," he said, grinning as he closed his eyes.

Then he opened them, glancing over to where Cassie was nestling in against a tree trunk while she spread out her beige bedspread-skirt all around her. "Remember, though," he said, "I'm not much of an artist."

"Ssssh!" Cassie said, with her finger to her lips. "You might hear yourself say that and actually think it's true! Of course you are an artist. Anyone who can create something as absolutely dazzling as that new stage of ours is nothing less than an artist of the first rank! Besides," she went on, "if you tell yourself you're artistic, you're bound to become more of an artist than if you tell yourself you're not! It's the same with telling yourself you're excited about something—or happy. There's nothing we believe more, dear bunnies, than the things we tell ourselves! Do you believe that?"

Rob smiled to himself and studied the interesting patterns thrown by the shadows of the trees across the sunken roof.

"It's like with me," Cassie sighed, smoothing the folds in her skirt as she went on talking almost absent-mindedly. "I could never quite be sure if I was a princess or not, so I just decided I might as well act like one anyway!"

"And you *are* a princess!" Brittany cried out. "I just know you are!"

Again Rob caught himself smiling as he bravely dipped his brush into a circle of rich brown. His eyes caught

Ashley's and he knew that they, too, believed Cassie was a princess — of some kind at least.

The art exhibit was held just before the sun went down. "A resounding success!" Cassie called it, even though no one but the five amateur artists themselves attended. Each painting had its own unique style: Rob's was bold and architectural, with heavy dark outlines emphasizing the angular structure of the surrounding trees as well as the cottage; Ashley's was much paler and more delicate, the trees becoming lacy wisps of light green; lively and full of color, Brittany's interpretation focused on the swerves and swirls of the branches and a cottage so full of life and vitality that it almost seemed human; and Tiger had chosen to make both the cottage and the trees less important than the delightful string of recognizable people he lined up in the foreground — including not only the five of them, but Nicholas, Cow, all four puppets, a nest of birds and a string of fish as well.

At the urging of the others, Cassie had agreed to attempt an abstract version, and although there were a few giggles at the simplified shapes and imaginative use of colors, they all had to finally agree that the unique arrangement of lines, textures, and shades was surprisingly delightful. And even Tiger, who had gasped, "Is that supposed to be our cottage?" when he first saw the results, decided he liked it best of all when Cassie told him she had simply been having the time of her life shifting and rearranging nature's shapes and colors until she found something quite unique that pleased and excited her.

While the sun slowly made its way downward toward the blue-green hills, its mellow light eased through the branches in warm, golden patterns on their play rehearsal. Birds chirped vigorously in the trees as though auditioning for a part, and even butterflies and an occasional dragonfly fluttered onto the stage as if to catch a sneak preview of the performance.

When the light finally grew dim and Cassie and the others disappeared into the cottage to prepare the supper, Rob stretched out lazily on the floor of the new stage, waiting for the first star to appear in the deepening blue of the sky overhead. His mind drifted back to the wintry days he and Brittany had painfully watched their mother suffering from a brain tumor, followed by the long difficult days when the stepfather he'd never liked had been tried and then sent to prison for embezzlement. And his thoughts shuffled through the unsettling period he and Brittany had spent as foster children of the Millers, to their eventual separation—Brittany to the Oglethorpes and he to live with the Helmeses—and finally to these incredible days of hummingbirds and dragonflies, of rhubarb and watercress, jasmine and sandalwood, Srinagar and Timbuktu, Rembrandt and Robert Frost . . .

A sudden rustling in the leaves nearby startled him. It was Ashley, her eyes anxious and troubled even in the waning light, and her voice lost in a frantic attempt to catch her breath.

"What is it?" he asked, sitting up.

"Oh, Rob, look! Look what I just found!"

She quickly spread out a wrinkled scrap of newspaper on the stage and then struck a match, her hand shaking.

"What is it?" he asked.

"While Tiger was helping Cassie get a fire started, he found these newspaper articles—the ones you had clipped out about us—and I guess he thought they were just old pieces of newspaper, but—"

"Did he burn them?" Rob interrupted, puzzled.

"No, because I caught him—just as he was starting to crumple them up," Ashley said, still trying to catch her breath.

"So?" Rob questioned.

"It isn't that—ouch!" Ashley said, giving the match a quick shake just as the flame was about to burn her fingers. Striking another one, she went on: "It's this— on the back of one of the articles about us. I just happened to see it—and I—I haven't shown it to anyone—yet."

Rob's eye caught the bold-print heading of the news-paper article illuminated by Ashley's match:

## Corbridge Hospital Patient Still Missing after 11 Days

**FAIRMONT, Dayton County—A 71-year-old mental patient, missing since May 8 when she walked away from the Cor-**

> bridge Sanatorium, is still reported missing after eleven days.
> After a week of searching turned up no clues to the patient's whereabouts, authorities feared that Selma Denner, believed to be a retired schoolteacher, may have suffered an accident or even become victim of foul play.

The match went out and Rob helped Ashley light the last one. Then they went on reading:

> Recent events, however, have given police reason to believe that the missing woman may still be somewhere in Dayton County.
> According to Mrs. Bessie Montague of Chesterton with whom the patient stayed for three months prior to being committed to the sanatorium, miscellaneous household items have been regularly disappearing from her home during the past week.

The flame of the last match sputtered and then went out.

CHAPTER

*20*

They knew, when it rained the next morning, that the days at Crumbledown would not last forever.

A sad feeling swept over Brittany the moment she opened her eyes, and she knew it had something to do with the startling news about Cassie that Ashley had nervously shared with her the night before. But there was something more – something she couldn't quite identify – something that had to do with the kind of feelings you get when you realize that Christmas Day is almost over or when Sunday afternoons begin to fade into evening.

Tiger felt the difference the minute he opened his eyes and saw that Cassie was still lying on the grass mattress beside them where she had fallen asleep the night before. Wasn't it the first morning at Crumbledown she hadn't awakened him with the music-box sound of her voice as she whirled about the room scattering flowers and sunshine around her? He looked at Cassie still lying asleep on the grass mat. Was that the secret thing that Rob, Ashley, and Brittany didn't want to share with him last night? Was Cassie sick?

For Rob, too, it may have been the quietness of the

cottage that awoke him, and as he sat up in bed beside Tiger and listened to the slow steady breathing of Ashley and Cassie — as well as the constant drip-drip of rain spiraling down through the holes of the roof — he knew it was all going to be changed. He'd felt nervous and anxious the night before at the discovery they'd made concerning Cassie's mental condition, but that same news this morning only left him feeling hollow, empty, and alone.

Ashley was the last of them to stir, and as she rolled over and blinked, she too sensed the sad, gray bleakness hanging over the quiet cottage. Lying on her side, she let her eyes gradually focus on the stub of candle with its unlighted wick barely peeking out of a circle of hard wax just a few inches from her head. Since Cassie had not been able to find another candle at Bessie Montague's, was there even enough of their candle left to last one more night? She felt something tighten inside her like a fist. It was true, wasn't it: their happy days at Crumbledown, just like the candle, were melting almost away.

Ashley rolled over. Not far away, Cassie's long hair spilled out across the floor boards like rivers of liquid silver. Instinctively, Ashley reached out her hand and let her fingers glide lightly along the waves of one of the thick strands of hair. Could it be true? Oh, how could it be true that Cassie was —

Her mind refused to say the word.

How could it be? If Cassie was — was really — *crazy* then what did that mean? What did anything mean?

Cassie stirred, and Ashley realized that she had let her fingers unconsciously tighten in the long tangle of hair. But Cassie's dark eyes were sparkling as soon as the lids fluttered open and, without a word, she immediately reached out her warm hand and enclosed Ashley's smaller, colder one.

But then the eyelids fluttered again and she raised herself up. "Amazing," she said. "Absolutely amazing!" She looked around as if in unbelief. "I've slept through all the roosters and meadowlarks and even the sunrise!"

Rob looked at her for a moment, trying hard to manage a smile but finding it difficult. "I don't think there even *was* much of a sunrise to catch this morning." Pushing aside the crooked piece of plywood covering the window, he stared off into the bleak grayness outside.

"Didn't the sun come up today?" Tiger asked, wide-eyed.

"Oh, well," said Cassie, "it probably pretended — enough at least to not throw the rest of the world off. But I'm certain it's been waiting — just especially for me!"

"Oh, Cassie," Brittany suddenly cried, throwing herself against Cassie and hugging her. "I'm afraid it's all going to end!" She kept her eyes squeezed shut, trying not to remember, to even believe, the horrible thing Ashley had whispered to her about Cassie before they'd gone to bed.

Tiger straightened up, still kneeling. "You mean the summer's over already?"

"Oh, no, little loves!" Cassie crooned dramatically. "Summer isn't over. In fact, it really hasn't even begun! And besides," she went on radiantly, "it never really *has* to end. Don't you know? You *make* summer in your hearts!"

Rob and Ashley exchanged sad glances, then noticed that Cassie, her eyes aglow, was looking intently into each of their faces. "Now, winter, my sweet ones — winter is positively lovely, and I must admit that I love every sparkle of the frost on the branches — and I simply go wild in the fall when the leaves sneak into their different-colored costumes — and I'm madly in *love* with foggy days! But, nevertheless, every once in a while, a day will creep in that I'm just not quite ready for — and that's when I have to use my magic."

She reached out her hand and touched Tiger's cheek. "Even you, sweet Tigedore — you can do it too! Remember — imagination! You simply bring back the summer by closing your eyes and thinking sweet peas and hollyhocks. Try it!" And pointing in turn at each one of them, she cried out: "Sing me a sunburst! Whistle me a rainbow! Laugh me fields of buttercups! Whisper me a butterfly!"

Tiger snickered, and Cassie went on: "You all can do it. Just remember what dear old Henry David taught us: more wonderful even than carving statues and painting pictures is being able to create the very *atmosphere* around us!"

"Then what shall we create for today?" Brittany asked. "Sunshine?"

"Whatever you wish!" Cassie twittered back. "We have our choice: we can bring back the blue skies in our minds or relish the actual rain-drops! But whatever we do, loves," she went on, her voice dropping to a whisper, "we must do it completely!"

"Let's relish the rain-drops!" Tiger cheered, then he stopped: "But do we even *have* any relish?"

Brittany and Cassie burst into laughter, but Ashley felt Rob touch her arm. "Did you—did you say anything to Tiger?" he whispered. "About—you know—?"

Ashley shook her head sadly. "I just couldn't."

Rob chewed on his lower lip as he watched Brittany and Tiger noisily jumping up to follow Cassie.

"I wish I hadn't even told Brittany," Ashley went on quietly.

"I know she won't let herself believe it," Rob whispered back. He hesitated. "I guess I don't want to believe it either."

"Let's just pretend—for now at least—that it isn't true," Ashley pleaded.

Rob looked down, trying to think, even though Tiger was calling to him to get up and go with them. "Well— I guess, for their sake at least—we can try to play along with it—for a little while." He looked up at her sadly just as Tiger ran and tugged at both of them.

"Come on, you guys! It's just *rain!* Let's enjoy it!"

Rob squeezed Ashley's hand and soon they were all up, running for the door and racing and leaping through the damp grass with arms outstretched and their faces upturned to the fresh, cool rain. They somersaulted, they cartwheeled, they spun around and whirled and rolled until, laughing and tumbling over one another, they felt like part of the spring rain themselves.

Cassie, soaked until her hair stuck to her forehead and cheeks, sang at the top of her voice while she danced in and out of the thicket of trees. Twice Rob slipped and fell into the stream as they carried out a wild and wet game of tag through the woods, and before long everyone had toppled in at least once, whether by accident or for the sheer fun of it.

While the rain pelted them more heavily than ever and Rob and Ashley followed Cassie along the stream to search for watercress, Brittany and Tiger lagged behind to make damp crowns of wild daisies. It was not long, however, before both of them, hugging themselves and shivering, looked at each other and stuttered, almost in unison: "Do you w-want to go b-b-back to the house?" Without answering, Tiger and Brittany linked hands and the two of them quickly fled back down the hill and across the little meadow to the cottage.

It felt a little warmer—and certainly much dryer— when they first stepped inside, but even as they huddled together under the one blanket, the shivering and teeth-chattering refused to stop. "Can we please m-m-make a fire?" Tiger finally stammered.

Brittany was ready to shake her head when she remembered that all the windows were covered but one. "Okay—if you'll help me block the window so nobody can see us." And they clutched the blanket around them with one hand while they busily fitted the homemade partition into the window, throwing the room into almost total darkness. Brittany searched for the matches on the rocky mantel and, together, they built a small but cozy fire.

How much time passed, neither one was quite sure, but they had changed into dry clothes, made two new puppet costumes, and started work on a new show when they heard the noise outside. They both immediately sat up straight and looked at each other. Although they had been half-listening for sounds of the others coming back to the cottage, the sound they heard above the crackling of the fire and the steady drip-drip on the roof was something else. Not wanting to believe what she thought it was, Brittany slipped nervously to the window and pulled back the covering far enough to peer outside.

There was nothing to see in front of the house. The rain was only a drizzle now, and a low mist hung close to the hill across the way. Then, out of the corner of her eye, she saw it.

She held her breath as she pressed the side of her face against the window frame to get a better glimpse of the movement just beyond the log that blocked the abandoned road. Two police cars were stopped at the end of the road, and cautiously passing in front of them now were three uniformed policemen.

Her voice caught in a little gasp as it suddenly occurred to her what they had done wrong. The chimney! The smoke! The blocking of the windows, she remembered in horror, had been to keep the firelight from being visible at night, but now, by daylight, there had been no darkness — nothing at all — to hide the smoke.

"Oh, no," she wept, covering her mouth with both her hands.

"What is it?" Tiger whispered, terrified.

"Come!" Brittany cried in desperation.

Tiger let her grab his hand and, without explanation, followed her, remembering how, not too many nights before, he and Ashley had done almost the very same thing.

Together they ran to the back door, but a noise outside froze them into a halt just as they also heard something push against the front door.

"Come!" Brittany shrieked under her breath, and they knocked open first the back door and then the warped screen door and fled out into the grayness, catching just out of the corner of their eyes a tall policeman not more than a few feet behind them.

"Stop!" they heard him yell above the pounding in

their ears, but they ran, with all their hearts, through the tall, wet grass into the fields beyond.

A wailing sound came from Tiger as, hand in hand, they almost flew across the long green stretch. But the shouting behind them grew louder as the rapidly approaching thud of footfalls resounded in their ears. Still crying out as he tried to look back over his shoulder, Tiger suddenly stumbled and went sprawling forward across the damp grass. Brittany too went down on one knee as he fell, but hearing the policeman at her back, screamed and let go of Tiger's hand as she pulled herself up and ran.

"They've got Tiger!" a voice from inside her head seemed to cry, but she wanted to cover her ears and her eyes and her mind and make it all go away. Her lungs burned and tears blurred her eyes as she fled, while behind her someone was still shouting and running and her head was pounding and pounding and pounding . . .

Coming down the hill where the trees followed the stream, Rob and Ashley echoed the words of a Swiss folk song after Cassie first sang out each line. Loaded with watercress and fresh flowers, they had almost forgotten their damp clothes and dripping hair. The trees thinned out and they found themselves at last coming down the last grassy slope on the hillside overlooking Crumbledown.

It was Rob who stopped first. "Hold it!" he whispered, reaching out an arm to stop the others. "Look!"

Two police cars were parked near the fallen log where the last traces of the road came to an end. The front door of the cottage was ajar and smoke—the three of them gasped almost at once!—came from the chimney.

"We've been discovered!" Ashley breathed, letting the flowers drop onto the ground.

Just then a faraway cry caused them to glance off in the distance where two policemen in tan uniforms came across the fields bringing with them two children. Cassie made a little sound and turned back suddenly toward the trees.

*Run!* Rob wanted to say—but it was too late. A third policeman had suddenly appeared in the doorway and, spotting them, called out something loudly as he started running briskly toward them.

Ashley felt her knees dissolving. *It's over,* a voice wept inside her head.

The days at Crumbledown were over.

# CHAPTER
## *21*

$A$shley had been sitting there by the window for a long time. Once in a while, a branch outside would quiver slightly because of a breeze or maybe even a bird, but then everything would go back the same as it was before. Nothing moved; nothing made a sound.

The window faced onto a small rectangle of grass at the back of the building. There were three slender trees that grew so feebly it was hard to tell whether they were just beginning to get their leaves or losing them. *It's funny,* Ashley thought. *It looks more like fall than spring.* And it did seem as if the summer had already gone, had shriveled and withered and crumbled into dust like a dead leaf. Of course, if Cassie had been there, she would immediately have sung the praises of even dead leaves — pointing out the subtle shades of grays and browns and autumn rusts and the intricate lacy patterns left when everything on the leaf had disintegrated except the delicate spidery frame.

Ashley felt something catch in her throat — something between a sob and a sigh — and she turned away from the window. It had only been five days since the police had taken them away from the cottage — but those five days seemed like forever. How could it be, she wondered, that the time they had spent at Crumbledown — all the wonderful days and hours and minutes — had begun to evaporate in her mind as quickly as a dream. It *had* really happened, she kept telling herself, and yet —

She heard the door click open and looked up to see Mrs. Rigby, one of the social workers, peeking in.

"Oh, hello," the lady said in a voice that tried to be cheerful. "I wondered where you were. Are you waiting for someone?"

"My brother," she answered. Then: "Well, not really my brother. He's actually Brittany's brother. Tiger — I mean Theodore — is mine. But we're all sort of brothers and sisters."

"Yes, I know," Mrs. Rigby said kindly. For a moment there was a silence and Ashley found herself looking down at the floor. She had come to the waiting room right after they had told her that Mr. and Mrs. Helmes were bringing Rob by to see them. She had left Tiger and Brittany working with clay at one of the long tables in the craft room.

"I understand that you're going on a little — excursion — ?" Mrs. Rigby tried, softly.

Ashley nodded.

There was another pause, then Mrs. Rigby spoke again. "Would you like to tell me about it?"

Ashley looked up. "I don't really know much. They just told me that Rob called to say that the family he lives

with would like to come and get us for a little while."
She crossed her feet and rubbed one of her sneakers
against the other. "Do you think," she said, suddenly
looking at Mrs. Rigby, "do you think maybe we're all
going to be living at the Helmeses?"

"I think not," the lady answered. "It's a—a matter
of space, really. They're willing to keep your brother—
Robert, that is. But—"

"Then will we have to go back to the Oglethorpes'?"
Ashley asked quickly.

"No—not necessarily. They've asked to have two or
three children again—but I think we would want to make
sure that you all—that everyone—felt—"

"Oh, please—don't send us back there. Especially not
after being with Cassie—"

Mrs. Rigby reached out and touched her hand. "What
a brave girl you were—and to think of you surviving out
there in the woods for almost two weeks on just berries
and—"

Ashley stared at her. Surviving? How could she tell
her? How would she make anyone understand that every
meal at Crumbledown had somehow become a delicious
feast that she wanted to remember for the rest of her
life?

"—and that poor old Denner woman," the social
worker was saying, "so old and frail, and not even in her
right mind—"

Ashley squeezed her eyes shut. Oh, Cassie, dear Cassie—will no one ever know how really wonderful you were?

The door to the waiting room clicked open and Brittany peeked in. "Haven't they come yet?"

Tiger's head poked in under Brittany's arm. "Will Cassie be with them?"

"Come in and sit with us," Mrs. Rigby invited, pulling Tiger over to sit by her. "Do you mean the Denner lady?" she asked, trying to answer the question. "I'm afraid not. In fact, I'm not sure we even know where they've taken her."

Brittany stopped, just as she was about to sit down. Did no one know where Cassie was? No longer focusing on the room, her eyes envisioned Cassie in a long flowing gown, pedaling furiously on Lancelot with her skirts and scarves floating behind her. "Did she run away again?" she asked anxiously.

"No, my dear," Mrs. Rigby said. "I'm quite certain that, wherever she is, she's being watched quite carefully this time."

"Would they—would they even lock her up?" Brittany asked, feeling a shiver as she pronounced the dreaded words.

"Well," Mrs. Rigby said, "I suppose—if they had to. You must realize that she is, after all, a very, very *strange* lady."

"If you think something's weird," Tiger said in a low mumble, "it's because you don't really understand it."

Ashley and Brittany almost wanted to leap from their seats and hug him, but just then the receptionist for the Child Protection Center stepped in to say that the visitors had arrived. And before she could move out of the way, the three of them, spotting Rob behind her, almost knocked her down as they ran, throwing their arms around him and breaking into sobs.

He squatted down and pulled them all in toward him. He didn't cry, but for a moment he just closed his eyes and didn't speak.

"Did you go back to school, Robbie?" Brittany sniffed. "We didn't even have to, since they were getting out for summer vacation this Friday anyway."

"You would have been celebrities at school," Rob said. "But it got awfully boring answering everybody's questions."

Noticing that Mrs. Rigby was introducing herself to Mr. and Mrs. Helmes, Rob stood up and took over the introductions of Ashley, Brittany, and Tiger himself. "*They're* my family now," he said, pulling Tiger in close against him. "And whoever takes one of us has to take us all."

He saw his foster parents exchange an embarrassed glance with the social worker, but he knew that what he said was true.

"If only we had a bigger house—" Mrs. Helmes offered.

"I really probably shouldn't bring it up until it's more

sure," Mrs. Rigby said, "but there is a slight possibility that we might have a new family that could take three or four—"

"Could they take five?" Tiger cut in, excitedly. In fact, how about six or seven, he thought to himself as he quickly tried to add on Nicholas and Cow and—

"It's all very unsure," Mrs. Rigby was saying. "But we're working on a way to let the four of you be together."

"Oh, that would be so perfect!" Brittany said. Then she added, "Well, *almost* . . . "

"Well, I'm sure you're all anxious to be on your way," Mrs. Rigby went on, talking to the Helmes couple. "So should we expect them back about six? Dinner at the Center is—"

"No problem," Mr. Helmes said. "We'll just keep them a couple of hours or so—maybe take them out for ice cream or something," he reassured her.

"Just one minute," Rob interrupted, stepping into the hall with Mrs. Rigby and talking to her with his back toward Ashley, Brittany and Tiger. They watched him gesture with his hands, then saw, in turn, Mrs. Rigby shrug and motion down the hall. While the Helmes couple attempted to maneuver them toward the front door, they looked back to see Rob talking next with the receptionist and then with Mrs. Pollock, the supervisor, who had just appeared in the doorway of the main office.

When he finally rejoined them, they heard him tell the Helmeses, "I just needed to find out something." And with no more explanation, they all stepped out into the cold, cloudy afternoon.

"So where will it be?" Mr. Helmes asked after everyone was settled in the car.

"We promised Rob that he could take you all out somewhere for an afternoon," Mrs. Helmes explained to the three young passengers in the back seat, "so—it's whatever you want—a movie, a snack at the drive-in—"

"First," Rob began, as he shifted Tiger's weight on his lap, "first, I want to go to Fairmont..."

"Fairmont?" Mr. Helmes asked, sounding bewildered. "That's forty-five minutes away. What in the world—"

"I know it's far," Rob put in cautiously, "but you did say that we could do anything—didn't you? It's very important—to all of us." He glanced at Ashley and Brittany and gave Tiger a little hug.

"Is it—is it Cassie?" Brittany whispered anxiously.

Rob gave his head a quick little nod, then announced to the couple in the front seat: "The lady at the Center says she thinks Cassie du Maurier is at the Corbridge Sanatorium in Fairmont."

Mrs. Helmes turned her head to stare at Rob. "But—but if she's really mentally ill—" she began.

"Mrs. Helmes," Rob said, pausing for just a moment to find the words he wanted, "if—if Cassie du Maurier is really crazy—then it's too bad the whole world can't be like that."

The Helmeses, their faces puzzled, both looked at Rob in silence. Finally Mrs. Helmes opened her mouth to speak, but her husband cut her off: "There's no way in the world you're going to get her out of there—and for all we know, they won't even let you visit her."

"But we *have* to try," Ashley urged.

"We've got to!" Brittany added.

"Please!" Tiger begged.

Mr. Helmes glanced at his wife, fidgeted nervously with his shirt collar, then, casting one final worried glance into the back seat, started the engine. Cheers broke forth from behind his back as the car pulled out into the gray day.

When they found Corbridge Sanatorium, it was a long, low, pink building in the trees. They parked in the small parking area nearby and all walked past the dried-up oval fountain in front of the French doors that opened first onto an entrance hall and then into a large room where a heavy nurse with dyed-red hair sat at a desk.

"Cassandra who?" she snorted when the two girls both pronounced the name almost at once.

"Or maybe Denner," Rob tried. "Selma Denner."

"*Selma Denner,*" the lady echoed with a knowing nod. Then her eyes darted back and forth at the eager group crowded around her desk. "You're not—well, of course you are!"

"We're her grandchildren!" Brittany said.

The nurse shot her an icy glance. "Then you've got the wrong Selma Denner," she murmured sarcastically, "because this Selma Denner never had a husband *or* children, let alone grandchildren."

"But we really are—" Ashley started.

"Listen, I know very well who you are. We *do* take time to read the papers around here." She seemed to fake a semi-polite smile, then looked them over until her eyes finally rested on Rob. "I must say—you look like an awfully big boy to have been kidnapped by a frail old woman!"

Rob opened his mouth to speak, but Brittany cried out first: "We were *not* kidnapped!"

"And we weren't involved in any kind of burglary ring, either," Ashley spoke up, "no matter what that one newspaper made it sound like."

"Ssh!" the nurse said, getting to her feet. "I don't care what you did or didn't do, but don't want you disturbing the patients. This *is* a hospital—"

"But can we see her?" Brittany urged impatiently.

"Can we?" Tiger begged.

"Well, certainly not all of you," the nurse snapped back.

"*We* don't need to go in," put in Mr. Helmes who had been hovering with his wife in the background. "We can just wait here for them—or out in front."

But even when the Helmeses stepped aside, the nurse went on scowling. "There's still too many of you—

and, besides that, I don't even know yet if she can receive visitors at all. She's a very sick woman—and, for all I know, she's still undergoing tests and can't be—"

"But can you check?" Rob interrupted.

The lady tugged at the white uniform stretched tightly across her bulging front. She flipped a page or two in the ledger laying open on her desk, snapped, "Take a seat," then turned and strutted down a dimly lighted hallway.

A few minutes later she waddled back. "She's been taking treatments all morning and she's very tired."

"But can't we even—" Rob started to say.

The nurse rolled her eyes like someone about to pass out. "I'm telling you she probably won't even recognize you. She's been heavily—"

"Oh, please!" Tiger pleaded.

The nurse sniffed, glared at them, then finally held up one plump finger. "One," she said flatly. "One of you can go in—that's all."

"One at a time?" Rob asked.

"One—*period,*" she growled emphatically. "*Uno, ein*—"

"I think Cassie's been teaching her languages," Tiger whispered, and the nurse glared at him.

"Just one?" Ashley asked, disappointedly.

Their hearts sank. Rob looked at them nervously. "Let me go," he said gently. "Okay? Maybe I can figure out something . . ."

The nurse, turning her head now to glare at Rob,

made a funny little snort, then turned around abruptly and marched down the hallway, Rob trailing behind. In front of a wide door, the nurse stopped, unlocked it with a key she took from the pocket of her white uniform, then proceeded down another hall. Still following, Rob peeked into each room as they went. In one of them, two old men in pajamas played cards while another sat staring out of the window. In another, a wrinkled old lady busily picked lint off her shawl, stopping long enough to mumble something and wave feebly at him as he passed by. In still another, an old man muttered to himself as he paced back and forth between the beds. Finally the buxom nurse halted at the end of the long hall, motioned brusquely toward an opening, and then waddled off around the corner.

Rob hesitated at the doorway. The room was a large one with four or five beds. In one of them a very thin and sickly lady with white hair lay watching TV. A few feet away an even older and thinner woman sat gripping the arms of a wheelchair, her frail neck craned forward as she too stared at the TV. Rob felt sick, afraid that one of them might be a ghostly version of Cassie. His eyes darted around the dim room. There was only one other figure — so bald, except for a few wisps of white hair, that he couldn't tell if it was a man or a woman — and it huddled on the floor nodding its head back and forth and making a funny clicking noise with its mouth. He felt cold shivers down his back. None of these were Cassie—none of them could *possibly* be her.

And then he saw her.

She was standing against the window where the blinding light was coming in, but he knew in an instant that the gray silhouette was hers. She was wearing her lavender gown and her hair hung in a long loose braid over one shoulder where she seemed to be fumbling with the end of it. He walked slowly across the room toward her.

She seemed to be staring out of the window, and she was singing softly to herself. Though the words almost sounded foreign, Rob thought he could hear something about "willows." He stepped to the window, a few feet in front of her, waiting for her to shift her eyes and recognize him.

She immediately stirred, but her eyes strangely seemed to pass over him. "Oh, my," she mumbled, touching her brow with one hand. "There was something I was going to do." He shivered. Her eyes now seemed to stare off blankly into the room.

"Cassie," he heard himself say weakly. But the words didn't seem to reach her.

"There was something . . . ," she murmured to herself. "What was it?" Then she turned, suddenly reaching out a hand to steady herself, as though dizzy.

"Cassie," he whispered again, this time to himself, for she had already begun to make her way slowly across the room. He watched her as she hesitated just a moment, and then she disappeared through the doorway.

Rob felt empty walking back to the reception area, and when Ashley, Brittany, and Tiger jumped up and ran over to him, he had to fumble for the right words to tell them.

"Can I see Cassie? Please?" Tiger pleaded.

Rob hesitated, then found the words: "She—she wasn't there."

"But where was she?" Ashley wanted to know.

"She—I don't know," he said. "Maybe they're still giving her—treatments—or tests or something."

Ashley looked around disappointedly. Except for the four of them, the reception room was now empty. Dejected, she sat down on one of the cushioned chairs. Then she looked up at Rob.

"There was a lady here a minute ago," she began, "one of the other nurses—and I guess she knows Cassie pretty well. But do you know what she told us? Not only is her real name not Cassandra du Maurier, but she's never been an actress—at least not a famous one. She's from somewhere in Ohio—and she used to be a school teacher."

She sank back in the chair. Ever since that night that Cassie had whirled into their lives, she had longed to rummage through albums and scrapbooks from long ago in search of a photograph, a theater program, or a newspaper clipping, anything that might give her a glimpse of the young Cassandra du Maurier. But now something inside made her ache even more—for no matter how she searched, there would be nothing to find. And yet—the thought almost made her want to search even more in hopes that somehow, somewhere—

"Cassie!" Tiger suddenly shrieked. "It's Cassie!"

He broke away from them and ran across the reception room to where a window looked out onto a little walled-in courtyard.

"It's Cassie!" he cried, rapping his knuckles on the window.

"Don't!" Rob called out, hurrying to him. "Come away," he said, lifting him away from the glass, as Ashley and Brittany crowded in against the window and stared out at the little square of grass and two or three fruit trees. There, just sitting down in a wicker chair under one of the trees, was Cassie.

"It *is* Cassie!" Ashley cried out.

They saw her look up as they tapped impatiently against the glass. Rob swallowed, seeing the same emptiness in her expression that he had seen down the hall. Only now there was something just a little different: she still looked puzzled and dazed, yet, as she slowly raised each hand to her temples and then narrowed her eyes as if trying to see better, there was a faint look on her face of someone trying to wake from a dream.

With one hand she steadied herself on the arm of the large wicker chair, and very slowly she rose and moved toward them as if in a trance. *Do you know us, Cassie?* Rob wanted to ask. And his heart beat faster when he thought he caught a trace—just a sudden glint—of recognition on her face.

"I want to go to her!" Tiger cried out, breaking away and starting to run down the hall that ran along one side of the courtyard. But before Rob could stop him, he had collided with the long white-trousered legs of a doctor.

"What's this?" the doctor asked, catching Tiger's arm and bending down.

"I've got to see Cassie! Please, can we go see her?"

"Cassie?" the doctor asked.

"Selma Denner," Rob explained.

"Well—" the doctor began, hesitantly.

"She's in the garden," Brittany put in, pointing back to the window in the reception area.

The doctor looked at them. "Wait a minute—you've got to be the ones that disappeared from—"

"We lived with Cassie in the woods," Tiger told him, "and it was so great!"

The doctor ruffled Tiger's hair. "So you want to see her again, do you?"

"Yes!" he cried, echoed by the girls.

"She's one of a kind, Selma Denner," the doctor said

softly. "They just don't make them quite like her any-more." He straightened up and sorted through the keys dangling from a chain attached to his belt loop. "If she's in the garden, I can let you all see her for a few minutes. But you might find her still quite sluggish. She's been under heavy medication."

He turned and unlocked the wide door behind him and led them down the hall where, as they turned the corner, they passed the stocky nurse with the intense red hair. She stopped abruptly, hands on hips, and glared at them, but they all marched proudly by, trailing the doctor. They heard her give a little snort as they rounded the corner.

When the doctor left them at the French doors leading to the miniature garden, it was Tiger who ran first and threw his arms around Cassie. Rob held the girls back, waiting to see her reaction.

"Oh, my . . . ," was all Cassie could say for a few moments. "Oh, my . . . " But they saw a tear spill down one cheek as she pushed Tiger back far enough to study his face.

"Oh, little lamb," she said gently. "I thought you were lost." She touched his cheek and studied his face intently. "I looked and looked for you. What was it we were doing? Hunting for string, wasn't it? I meant to help you with the puppets — but I can't seem to find the scissors. I can't find anything. Nothing is quite where I —" She looked up and saw the other three faces. "How beautiful," they heard her whisper. "How perfectly beautiful you all are . . ."

She let herself drop back gently into the big wicker chair, then, smiling, she slowly reached out her arms, and they all ran to hug her.

"I can't seem to find Lancelot," she said, taking longer than usual to say each word. "I was going to go look for you all, but—I couldn't even find the tree where we . . . " Her voice trailed off. "I wonder if someone remembered to feed Nicholas . . . " she mumbled. Then she closed her eyes and seemed to sink back into the chair.

Ashley grasped Rob's arm and whispered anxiously: "Is she dying?"

"I—I think she's just dozing," he answered uneasily, carefully watching Cassie's slow, rhythmic breathing.

For several minutes they talked in whispers among themselves, but just as they were deciding whether to leave, her eyes opened suddenly and she sat up straight in the chair.

"Oh dear—I—I must have slept!" she said, her voice regaining some of the old bounce. "How perfectly rude of me!" She looked around, patted the back of her hair, and brushed some invisible crumbs from her lap. "What a terrible hostess I must be!"

Rob squatted down in front of her. "You're perfect," he said softly, "and we hope you'll never change."

"Never!" said Tiger, placing his hand on hers and patting it gently.

"Oh, but we simply must change—mustn't we?" she said, smiling more like the old Cassie. "If we aren't changing and growing every day—if we aren't always *becoming* instead of just simply *being*—well, wouldn't that be a terrible thing?"

"I know someone who's changed a whole lot since he met you," Rob said, taking her other hand in his.

"And I think I know three more," Brittany said, beaming at Ashley.

Ashley knelt down in front of her. "Cassie—" she began. "Oh, Cassie, are you happy?"

"Why, what a question, love!" Cassie answered. "Can you imagine Cassandra du Maurier *un*happy?"

"No!" Tiger responded.

Ashley tried again, "But I mean—"

Cassie interrupted her as one of her trembling hands reached out to touch Ashley's lips. "If you want to know a deep secret, I'm really not terribly fond of this—this house. I scarcely know these people and—I must admit—I find them just a little dull." She leaned forward and lowered her voice. "Incredibly dull, if you want to know the truth. I'll swear none of them have ever run barefoot through the grass at dawn—or shouted Shakespeare from under a waterfall."

Tiger snickered. "Or imagined how the color redorange would dance if you turned it loose in the woods!"

"One day," Rob began, "one day, we're going to come

and get you, Cassie. I'm not sure how—or when—but we will—and that's a promise."

Cassie clasped his hands and whispered: "If you say it, sweet Robino, I know you'll do it." Her eyes rested fondly on each one of them and then she let herself lean back once more in the big fan-backed chair. "Dear me—I just wish whatever it is they feed me here wouldn't muddy up my thoughts so. I need some of that fresh air—morning air—to clear up the clutter. Up here," she said, tapping her temple.

"Is there anything we can get for you?"

Cassie smiled and closed her eyes momentarily. Then, opening them, she announced in a whisper. "Yes. Send me bouquets of meadowlarks! And," she added, "if you could somehow keep it in an envelope, you might just send me the song of the whippoorwill." She closed her eyes again. "Oh, my, I just remembered—there was the most exquisite little Jewish song about raisins and almonds that I always meant to teach you! Oh, well," she sighed, "we'll just have to save that for—for some other afternoon."

"Or for some *morning*," Brittany corrected.

"Oh, absolutely!" Cassie agreed, her eyes fluttering open as she leaned forward again. "Absolutely. Always, dear children, always remember to keep the morning and the springtime in you—will you promise me that?"

They all nodded.

Tiger nestled his head against her. "I don't want to leave you, Cassie!"

"Leave me?" Cassie asked, astounded. "Why, wherever you are, love, I'll always be there. I'm the grass, Walt Whitman used to say. Look for me under your boot soles. Oh yes, dear Tigedore, I'll always be there when you need me. My dear, dear children — have I taught you nothing? Think clover!" she said, looking at Rob. "Taste sunshine!" she told Tiger. "Sing me lilacs!" she said to Brittany. And then, for Ashley: "Whisper me a butterfly!"

They looked up to see the doctor standing in the opening between the French doors.

"I think we'd better let you rest, Selma," he said carefully.

"Poor dear," Cassie murmured to Rob with a faint smile. "He doesn't even know who I am."

"But *we* know," Rob whispered back, squeezing her hand. "Goodbye, Cassie," he said "And don't forget what I promised."

"Absolutely not, dear Robino," Cassie promised. Then: "Goodbye," she said softly, and, one by one, she kissed them all on each cheek.

Tiger was the last — and she lingered just a moment before she put her hands on each side of his face and kissed him gently on the forehead.

"Goodbye, little prince," she whispered.

They began watching for the lane just a few miles out of Fairmont, afraid they might not recognize it, coming from the other direction. But half an hour and hundreds of fields and farmhouses went by before the landscape began to look familiar. The clouds had gone now and the pasture land seemed fresh and green in the late afternoon sun.

"It's a white house — with green shutters, right?" Tiger asked.

"The cottage?" Rob asked.

"No," Brittany corrected, flashing a secret smile at Ashley. "The birthday house — where they always have birthday parties."

Tiger gasped. "Oh, this time can we really go — please?"

Mr. Helmes cast a puzzled glance over his shoulder. "A party? I promised the Center I'd have you back by six."

"It's only a joke," Ashley put in, and explained to Rob and the Helmeses what had happened that first rainy afternoon when they had left the school bus.

"I'll tell you what, Colonel Boo," Rob announced,

when Ashley had finished. "See that sack in the back window? Can you guess what's in there?"

Tiger twisted himself around on Rob's lap and stared at the the brown paper bag. "What is it?" he finally asked. "A present?"

"A present. But not for us," Rob added hastily. He reached back and pulled the sack down, opening it enough for Tiger to peek in.

"Chocolate cupcakes . . . " Tiger said, under his breath. "But who for?"

Rob explained that he had bought the cupcakes that morning after Mr. Helmes had told him that he would take them all anywhere they wanted to go for the afternoon. "Remember how we were always going to take something to the farmer and his family that owns Cow? It's not much for all the milk we drank—but at least it's something."

"Do we need to sneak up to their doorstep and—"

"No, Colonel Boo—no more sneaking and hiding. We'll just knock on their door."

"There it is!" Brittany suddenly shouted. "Isn't it?"

Mr. Helmes slowed the car as the four in the back seat peered intently from the side window to see the little frame house with the green shutters a few hundred feet down a dirt lane.

"That's it. That's the birthday house!" Ashley said, feeling a sense of nervous anticipation and wondering why they had missed the farmhouse and the little lane, even though they had looked for it, on their way to Fairmont earlier that afternoon.

"What do you say we just drive on, further down the highway," Rob asked, "and leave the cupcakes at Cow's farm, and then walk across the field from there to the cottage?"

It seemed right, Ashley agreed, to approach the cottage on foot — and although they had reached it the first time by following the little dirt lane and then turning off on the weed-covered road that led to the left, her memories now of coming home to Crumbledown in the evening were mainly memories of crossing the fields and ducking under the fences as they carried home the pail of milk, a handful of eggs, and occasionally mint leaves and watercress from the ditchbank.

"Go just a little farther . . . ," Rob directed, and Mr. Helmes drove the car slowly along the side of the road until they spotted the familiar farmhouse and barn surrounded by trees. Although the house looked quite different from the highway than it did from the fields behind it, they immediately recognized the barn.

"Could you leave us here," Rob asked, "and then pick us up in about twenty minutes at the end of that lane we passed back there? Just drive all the way down the lane until you can turn left, and then go down to where the road ends."

"If you'd rather, we could just wait here while you deliver the cupcakes and then drive you right there," Mr.

Helmes said, as if trying to be helpful. But the four in the
back seat quickly exchanged glances and knew that going
back to Crumbledown had to be a special kind of ritual:
they had to be alone — and they had to approach it on foot
through the grassy fields.

"It's better this way," Rob told the Helmeses softly,
and he helped the others climb out of the back seat onto
the roadside. And as the car turned around and started
slowly back down the highway toward the little lane, the
four of them walked down the dirt road and through the
gate that led to the sprawling farmhouse set back in the
grove of trees.

They felt both disappointed and relieved when no one
answered their repeated knocks on the screen door. "But
at least we can leave a note," Rob suggested. And with
the stub of a pencil found in the pocket of his jeans, he
printed carefully across the side of the bag:

> THANK YOU AND YOUR GOOD
> COW FOR SHARING YOUR MILK
> FOR A WHILE. IT NOT ONLY
> HELPED KEEP US ALIVE BUT MADE
> US FEEL GLAD THAT WE WERE.

And then they all signed their names — and Cassie's as
well.

"And don't forget to write Nicholas's name on there
too," Tiger reminded them, remembering all the times
he had thought about the poor white cat wandering by

himself in and out of the empty cottage after the police had taken them away.

They went around the back, cut through the barnyard past the pig pens and chicken coops and barn, then unhooked the back gate and went out into the field. There they found Cow waiting by the fence.

"Oh, I think she remembers us!" Ashley said, putting her arm around her and letting the cow's warm nose nuzzle her neck and cheek. "*Adios,* Cow," she whispered softly. "We can't stay long this time—but please don't forget us."

It seemed strange not to take time to look for eggs, but they felt their hearts beating faster as they ducked under the fences and jumped ditches as something continued to pull them toward the trees where the cottage would be.

"What—what if it's not there," Ashley suddenly found herself thinking aloud. They all stopped suddenly and stared at her.

"What do you mean?" Brittany asked.

"I can't see it," Ashley said, swallowing. "Can you? It's got to be there—but—but what if they tore it down?"

"What if—what if it was never there at all?" Brittany asked, her voice sounding very soft and very small.

"It's got to be there," Rob stated, but he found himself breaking into a run to prove that it really was there, somewhere, beyond the trees. The others ran through the tall grass behind him.

"There it is!" Ashley cried, catching a glimpse of the beige stone through the leaves, and they slowed down as, more and more, bits of walls, the chimney, the ramshackle roof, the door became visible through the greenery.

They stopped. In some ways it seemed more beautiful than ever: in just the five days they had been away, the vines on the cottage seemed to have almost doubled, accounting for why it had blended and almost disappeared into the surrounding foliage. But in another way, there was something sad about it, even from here. You could tell, Ashley felt, that no one was home, that it was almost how they had found it — abandoned, neglected.

They moved slowly, silently, toward it. The front door stood ajar, and Brittany found herself aching to see Cassie suddenly swirl through the doorway with bouquets of lilacs or wild daisies. An unexpected sound from inside startled her. There was a light thump, a faint "miao," and then Nicholas came trotting through the opening.

"Nicky!" Tiger squealed, gathering the streak of white fur up under his chin. "You waited for us! Look, Britt! Look, you guys! He almost growed up!"

Brittany pushed the door open all the way and stepped in. There was a dank smell — and puddles of water on the floor still left from all the rain. The beds had been torn up, the dried grass scattered; the bags of clothes and all other belongings were gone. Only a few dead flowers drooped like weeds over the edges of empty bottles.

In the little side room that had been Cassie's, Rob stooped to pick up the torn paperback copy of Robert Frost's poems and slipped it into his pocket. The house had a musty, mildewy smell, like a house not lived in for years.

Ashley slipped out the backdoor and into the sunshine, and Brittany followed her. Both knew what the other was feeling; they had wanted to find everything at Crumbledown still the same, and when it was not, something hurt down inside.

"Let's go down by the stream," Brittany suggested, and they walked through the heavy foliage — even more dense and green now after the heavy rains — to the secluded spot where so many games had been played and so many stories told. Bits of melodies and snatches of poetry still seemed to linger there. Names like Tchaikovsky, Van Gogh, and Wordsworth still seemed to reverberate through the trees.

*My journal,* Ashley thought, feeling a tinge of guilt. *I've got to start writing again.* What would Cassie think if she knew how the thick notebook and pencil had lain for days forgotten in a drawer at the Child Protection Center.

She turned to Brittany. "You didn't — you didn't leave your watercolors here, did you?"

Brittany shook her head. "The paints and the paper — they were just about the only things I took, except for the blue dress I was wearing. The policeman let me go back to the cottage and get them when Tiger got his puppets."

Ashley picked one of the few remaining berries from a bush and nibbled on it. There was a kind of gentle quiet, a peacefulness here, that she hated to leave. Her mother's face flashed unexpectedly before her, then dissolved. Strange, she thought. Had her mother ever known any place like this? Could she ever—some day—bring her here?

The sound of a car's engine approaching interrupted her thoughts. She looked up, knowing that, beyond the thick greenery, the Helmeses must be driving down the lane. A crackling of twigs made her look up and Rob and Tiger stepped into the grove of trees.

"The stage is still there," Rob said. He paused for a moment. "I'm sorry we never got to do your play." He hesitated again. "I guess I never got to tell you—-but it really *was* a good play."

For a moment there was only the sound of birds and crickets and the cool gurgling of the stream. "Listen," Brittany said, and they all felt a shiver ripple through them. Beyond the sounds of birds and crickets and water, there was a very faint yet distinct sound of someone singing.

"It's Cassie!" Brittany breathed.

Tiger squeezed Nicholas against him. "She said she'd be with us—wherever we are!"

Rob listened. "Wait!" he said, and listened again. It

was almost like the day they had stood there in the same shady glen and listened to Cassie dramatically rehearsing her part on the outdoor stage; only now, faint and far away, she was singing. He listened again.

He swallowed, almost hating to say it. "Do you know what it really is? It's just the sound of someone singing coming from the car radio. I'm sure now—because I saw the Helmeses car driving down the lane just as Tiger and I came to find you."

"But she *is* here at Crumbledown," Brittany said, trying not to feel disappointed. "Can't you feel her?"

"You know what?" Tiger announced suddenly. "I just feel like *staying* here." Meekly, he looked at the others in hopes they would agree.

"I'll tell you something," Rob started. "I had even thought of—of maybe running away again. In fact, if you want to know the truth, when I went to buy the cupcakes this morning, I kept imagining how we would have Mr. Helmes let us out at the farmhouse, and then, after we had delivered them, we'd sneak around the back and cut across through the fields and—"

"And never go back?" Ashley asked anxiously.

Rob swallowed. "I did think about that—and I even thought about it this afternoon, too. But now—"

"Now what?" Tiger asked.

"I don't think we ought to do it—anymore. We told the Helmeses we'd meet them out there by the log—and we have to do it—because we said we would. But—if we can just find a family where we can all be together—and if—*someway*—we can get Cassie out of that Sanatorium, then—"

"Exactly!" Ashley said.

"Absolutely!" Brittany echoed.

"Positively!" Tiger cried.

And they almost floated through the trees.